Danger Signals

KATHLEEN CREIGHTON

MILLS & BOON®
Pure reading pleasure™

*First published in Great Britain 2009
by Harlequin Mills & Boon Limited,
Eton House, 18-24 Paradise Road, Richmond, Surrey TW9 1SR*

© Kathleen Creighton-Fuchs 2008

ISBN: 978 0 263 87291 0

46-0509

*Harlequin Mills & Boon policy is to use papers that are
natural, renewable and recyclable products and made from
wood grown in sustainable forests. The logging and
manufacturing processes conform to the legal environmental
regulations of the country of origin.*

*Printed and bound in Spain
by Litografia Rosés S.A., Barcelona*

ABOUT THE AUTHOR

Kathleen Creighton has roots deep in the California soil but has relocated to South Carolina. As a child, she enjoyed listening to old-timers' tales, and her fascination with the past only deepened as she grew older. Today she says she is interested in everything – art, music, gardening, zoology, anthropology and history, but people are at the top of her list. She also has a lifelong passion for writing, and now combines her two loves in romance novels. Check her out at www.kathleencreighton.com.

This book is for the brothers and sisters
I've never met
And who don't know I exist.
Yet.
If the Fates allow,
I will find you...
Someday.

Prologue

In a house on the shores of a small lake, somewhere in South Carolina...

"Pounding...that's always the first thing. Someone—my father—is banging on the door. Banging...pounding... with his fists, feet, I don't know. Trying to break it down."

"And...where are *you?*"

"I'm in a bedroom, I think. I don't remember which one. I have the little ones with me. It's my job to look after them when my father is having one of his...spells. I have to keep them out of his way. Keep them safe. I've taken them into the bedroom and I've locked the door, except...I don't trust the lock, so I've wedged a chair under the handle, like my mom showed me. Only now I'm afraid, terrified even that won't be enough. I can hear the wood splin-tering…breaking. I know it will only take a few more blows and he'll be through. My mother is screaming…crying. I hold on to the little ones—I have my arms around them, and they're all trembling. The twins, the little girls, are sobbing and crying, 'Mama, Mama…' but the boys just cry quietly.

"I hear sirens…more sirens, getting louder and louder until it seems they're coming right into the room, and there are lots of people shouting, and all of a sudden the pounding stops. There's a moment—several minutes—when all I hear is the little ones whimpering…and then, there's a loud bang, so loud we—the children and I—all jump. We hold each other tighter, and there's another bang, and we flinch again, and then there's just confusion…voices shouting…footsteps running…glass breaking…the little ones crying…and I think I might be crying, too…"

"Oh, God…I'm sorry, Cory. It's all right…it's all right…I love you…I've got you…"

He discovered he *was* crying, but he also knew it was all right. *He* was all right. Sam, his wife, was holding him tightly, cradling his head against her breasts, and her hands were gentle as they wiped the tears from his face.

"I'm going to find them, Sam. My brothers and sisters. I have to find them."

Samantha felt warm moisture seep between her lashes. "Of course you do." She lifted her head and took his face between her hands and smiled fiercely at him through her tears. "We'll find them together, Pearse," she whispered. "We'll find them. I promise you we will."

Chapter 1

Portland, Oregon

Detective Wade Callahan had nothing against mind readers, or fortune-tellers, or whatever they were calling themselves nowadays. So long as they stuck to their tarot cards and beaded curtains and refrained from activities that might conceivably engage the interests of the bunko squad. As far as he was concerned, those so-called psychics had no business in a police squad room unless it was as a victim or perpetrator of a crime.

And, given the nature of their business, he figured one scenario was about as likely as the other.

They sure as hell had no business wandering around a crime scene. Particularly *his* crime scene.

For some reason the fact that this one happened to be a particularly attractive woman only made matters worse. What in the hell was the captain thinking? And who'd ever heard of a psychic with tousled sunshine hair and big, innocent blue eyes, freckles scattered across her rosy cheeks and pert little…

Ah, *hell*.

"You're growling again," Ed Francks said, giving him an elbow nudge in the ribs.

"Wasn't growling," Wade growled. "Muttering. That was muttering. There's a difference."

"Uh-huh." His former partner looked him over, eyebrows raised in mild rebuke. "Best get used to it, man. You heard what the captain said. She's part of the task force from now on." He shrugged. "Anyways, from what I hear this one could be the real deal."

Ed Francks was a Vietnam vet who'd seen too many young lives wasted in the jungles and rice paddies of the Mekong Delta and was spending his life making up for that by teaching young police recruits how to stay alive in the urban jungles of Portland, Oregon. He was a gentle bear of a man and a tough task master of a police sergeant and one hell of a fine police officer who, in Wade's opinion, should have been made detective long ago. And no doubt would have, if he'd wanted any part of it.

It had been a long time since Wade had been partnered with Francks, but he'd requested him for this task force because he had a fine analytical mind and more common sense than anybody else he knew, and was the person he most wanted watching his back when push came to shove. Which didn't mean he always agreed with him.

"Yeah, well, she looks more like a damn high school cheerleader than somebody that talks to dead people," Wade muttered. *Muttered, not growled.*

"That's not what she does." Francks had shifted unconsciously into his drill sergeant's pose—feet planted apart, arms folded on his chest. Now he tilted his shaved head toward the woman wandering—apparently aimlessly—around the section of park playground that had been roped off with yellow crime scene tape. "You heard her at the briefing. She picks up vibes. *Feels* things."

Wade made an ambiguous noise.

Francks looked over at him, black eyes reflecting sunlight in a way that turned them the color of dead ripe plums. "I don't know. Could be something in it. The way she explained it, she says all thoughts and emotions give off electrical energy—that's a proven fact—and it stands to reason intense emotions would give off a whole lot more energy. Like fear…rage…the kinds of things you'd expect from somebody involved in a crime, particularly a homicide. So, say there's all this energy floating around, it seems like there might be people, certain people, that are more sensitive to it, that could maybe pick up on it. Like, you know, the way dogs can smell things we can't." He stiffened his stance, as if to shore up his case. "Sounds possible to me."

Wade snorted—nothing ambiguous about it. "Come on."

"Look, all I know is, she's had some success working with other departments—Seattle, San Francisco, L.A.— and there was that kidnapping in Yreka last summer, she was involved with that. Hey, man, let's face it, we're not getting anywhere with these murders, and she lives right

here in Portland. Be pretty dumb not to give her a shot,
seems to me. What've we got to lose?"

"Credibility?" Wade said dryly. "Self-respect?"

He looked over at the woman. She was sitting in one of
the swings with her head down and her hands over her face.
She didn't look so much like a cheerleader now as a little
girl who'd lost her mommy.

Well, hell, he thought. *I've got to talk to the woman
sooner or later. Might as well be now.*

"Play nice," Francks called to him as he hitched his
jacket more squarely on his shoulders and stepped over the
curbing into the sandy playground.

Wade grunted.

Darkness...cold...so cold.

*Fear...paralyzing fear...can't think...should fight,
struggle...maybe if I could scream...I am screaming! Why
can't I hear myself screaming?*

*Don't hurt me! Please...don't hurt...don't hurt...no-
hurtnohurtnomorehurtpleaseplease...*

Oh God... No! No...no...

Can't be happening...not real...can't be real!

I can't die! Please...I don't want to die!

I don't understand...why are you doing this?

Why...why...why...

"Why...what?"

The voice was deep and flat, and came from somewhere
outside the terror that held her in its clammy web. Tierney
Doyle clung to the voice, used it like a lifeline and managed
to haul herself back to corporeal reality, the tangible, taste-

able, *seeable* world. As she struggled to focus on the tall
figure of the man standing in front of her she felt the reas-
suring hug of the swing seat around the backs of her thighs,
the warm Portland sunshine beating down on her head, the
bite of the steel chains she'd gripped so hard she knew there
would be red indentations and white ridges across her
fingers and palms when she let go.

She touched a toe to the depression in the sand beneath
the swing dug by small, pushing feet, making the swing
rotate slightly as she looked up, up, up, past the slightly
rumpled tan slacks, the darker brown sport jacket with the
Portland P.D. detective's badge pinned to the pocket, the
unbuttoned shirt collar and the hard, square jaw wearing a
hint of five o'clock shadow, though it was not yet noon. On
up to eyes the color of mountain lakes under cloudless
skies, with lashes any woman would die for.

"What?" she said vaguely as she met the look of cold
appraisal in those deep-blue eyes. *This* she recognized—
she'd seen that look often enough before. A skeptic, obviously, like so many in his line of work.

"Are you all right? You looked like you were about to
pass out." It wasn't an expression of sympathy; his mouth
hadn't softened, though there was a pleat of frown lines
between his dark brows.

*Skepticism, but compassion, too. Nice, even though he
doesn't look it.*

She tried to produce a smile, but it was too soon. *Too
soon.* "I'm fine," she murmured, and mentally added a determined, *I will be.*

She rose from the swing but kept one hand tightly on
the chain, uncertain of her legs. She brushed at the seat of

her pants and nodded in a way that took in the sandy play-ground, the children's play equipment incongruously painted in happy primary colors, and the people—not children, but grown-ups, dressed in muted shades of gray and tan and brown—moving purposefully among them. Like sparrows, she thought, foraging in a bed of flowers. "It gets to me sometimes, that's all."

"Yeah, crime scenes can be tough," the detective said, slipping a pair of sunglasses from his inside jacket pocket and putting them on. "Especially on civilians."

She glanced up at him, and this time she did smile. "You're not a believer in…what I do."

His eyebrows lifted in mock surprise. "Wow, you *are* a mind reader."

"I read emotions, not minds."

And he watched her eyes change, an effect so unmis-takable it startled him, but which he couldn't have de-scribed to save his life. A veil…a shadow…and yet, neither of those. Somehow, though they continued to gaze into his, her eyes seemed to be looking at something else, some-thing only she could see. He wanted to tell her to stop whatever it was she was doing. She was creeping him out. But before he could open his mouth, she spoke again, in a hoarse almost-whisper.

"He tortured her…tied her here—" she gestured toward the swing that hung limp and empty next to the one she clung to "—so her feet wouldn't touch the ground. He cut her, burned her…" And as she spoke the words in a breathy undertone her hand wandered here and there over her body, showing him *where*.

A strange prickling sensation washed over his skin. He

felt his stomach go cold. *How could she know that? No one outside the task force knows that—no one. And it wasn't covered in the briefing this morning, either.*

"Who told you that?" he demanded, his voice raw with anger. But she didn't seem to hear him.

"He covered her mouth with something—tape, I think— so she couldn't scream. Couldn't—" She let go of the chain suddenly and gripped his arm instead. He felt the cold of her hand through the layers of his shirt and jacket. The veil—whatever it was—was gone from her eyes and they focused on him again. "Please—I need to get away from it. From here. This place. Do you mind?"

"Sure," he said, "why not? Where do you want to go?"

He had to hand it to her—she was good. Damn good. The hand on his arm actually felt like it needed his support, and he could see tiny beads of sweat scattered across her forehead and the bridge of her freckled nose. He could hear the faint shudder of her uneven breathing. And even with her tousled head of sunshot red-gold curls just inches from his shoulder, he realized he hadn't thought of cheerleaders since she'd first looked into his eyes.

"I don't care, just—" She nodded toward the parking lot, crowded now with law enforcement and crime scene vehicles of all shapes and sizes. The news media, thank God, had been restricted to the park perimeter by manned police barricades. "Just anywhere. I need some distance. From where it happened."

"Sure. Whatever you say." Annoyance made him tight-lipped and shorter with her than he should have been, though the annoyance was with himself for beginning to believe, even for a moment, that there might be something to her flimflam. And for not being smooth enough to think of a way to rid his arm of the oddly disturbing weight of her hand without seeming churlish.

They walked, slowly. He had the interrogator's knack of patient waiting, and in due time it paid off. She began to talk, in a voice that seemed completely normal, nothing like the hoarse half whisper of a few minutes ago. She had a nice voice, he had to admit, with an almost musical lilt to it. Out of the blue he found himself wondering if she did sing, or play an instrument of some kind.

"I don't know if I've been able to pick up much—anything that will help you identify the killer, that is. She didn't know him. She was so afraid, at first. Later, she just wanted to know—she just kept asking *Why?* That was what was in her mind when she… At the end."

Wade let out a breath, shook his head. He couldn't believe what he was about to ask. "What about him? The killer? Pick up any vibes from him?"

There was a long pause before she answered, and this time while he waited he allowed himself to look down at her, thinking—hoping—he might get some kind of clue to what made her tick. He didn't, of course, but what he did get was an unexpected kick right square in the libido. *Damn,* but she was pretty, even with a little watermark frown marring the creamy perfection of her forehead.

She jerked a look up at him, as if she'd—*damn it,* he wasn't going to believe she'd read his mind.

But he saw a pink tinge in her cheeks before she looked away again.

"Yes," she said finally, with a small frustrated shake of her head, "but it's all confused. Muddled. I can't make sense of it. He's…he was in a terrible hurry, for one thing. And distracted, almost, as if his mind wasn't entirely on *her*—this victim. That really doesn't seem right, does it?"

He stopped walking, mentally gritting his teeth at the thought of what he was going to say next, and turned to face her. "Okay, how about this? Don't try to make sense of it. Just tell me what you saw. Uh, felt. Whatever."

She nodded, touched the fingertips of both hands to her lips and closed her eyes. "Fear. That's what he feels. He's afraid, like a child is afraid. And in a hurry. He must hurry…finish this. He wants it over with. He's not enjoying it. But he has to do it. *Has to.* He isn't seeing her. Or—he sees her, but she's all mixed up with…others. Other faces. I can't—"

"Other faces? His other victims, you mean?"

"I don't know…some of them, maybe. Yes, definitely some. But others…" She shook her head, opened her eyes and aimed them at him, and instinctively he threw up his emotional defenses to block against the pain and confusion he saw in them. "I don't remember seeing any of them at the briefing this morning."

"Could be more victims we haven't found yet…" He heard himself say the words, musing, half to himself, and couldn't believe it. His mind flashed a silent blasphemy.

She'd started walking again, but now she stopped and looked at him. "Uniforms. He's…I think he's afraid of uniforms."

Wade almost laughed, but snorted instead. Talk about obvious. Once again he'd almost bought it, whatever it was she was selling. "Cops, you mean? Well, he damn well better be," he said in the even tone he employed when he was on the verge of losing his temper. "Because we're going to nail this creep's ass."

Hopefully, he thought, before he kills anyone else.

Tierney stared at him, frowning a little.

Uniforms...cops...? No, that's not...it's something... something... Wait...I can't...

But it was gone, the emotions dissolving in her consciousness like smoke in the wind.

She studied the detective's profile, noting the narrowing of the eyes behind the dark glasses, the tension in the jaw. He was struggling with his disbelief, fighting hard to hold on to it. She didn't have to have The Gift to deduce that. But other than that...

I can't read him. He's shielding himself from me—which is proof he does believe, even if he doesn't know it yet.

Okay, except for that one moment, that blast of pure lust. He hadn't quite been able to shield that—few men could. She was used to that sort of response from men, but she didn't think she'd ever get over being embarrassed by it.

Probably she was just tired. Crime scenes always did that to her. The intensity of emotions—the pain, the fear, the rage and regret—sapped her energy the way a bout of the flu would, leaving her wobbly and light-headed. Utterly drained. She wanted—needed—to renew her soul. Maybe go up to the Rose Garden, to feed on the pure joy and simple beauty there. Or to the empty quiet, the complete absence of emotion that was her home so often these days...

The step was there unexpectedly, the step down from the curbing that separated the sidewalk from the parking lot. She didn't see it, wasn't ready for it, and it jarred the left side of her body all the way to her jaw. She stumbled and lurched forward, bracing for a humiliating fall. And instead felt a hand close hard around her upper arm.

At the same instant her mind felt the sting of profound emotional turmoil, like a slap in the face. It was a sense of loneliness and frustration and loss, and also of empty spaces, as if pieces of the man were missing, simply not there. It unnerved her, in that one brief moment before it was gone, and its going left her feeling oddly bereft and at the same time awed, as if she'd happened to catch a glimpse, just one silvery flash, of some extraordinarily rare and elusive creature.

"Are you all right?"

The detective was looking at her with that compassionate frown again, and she realized she had caught hold of his forearm and was clinging to it like a sapling in a hurricane. Lord only knew what he must have thought—that she'd injured something, sprained an ankle, probably.

She hastily let go of his arm and said, "Yes—yes, I'm fine—thank you—" her voice made jerky by the brushes and tugs she was making to her hair and clothing, setting herself to rights. "I didn't see that step. I'm sorry."

"No problem." His voice was the cop's, flat, devoid of all expression. So were his eyes, as he went on looking at her in that narrowed-down way cops have that can make even the most innocent of citizens feel guilty as sin. "Sure you're okay?"

"Yes. Really. I just…I think I'd like to go home now, if there's nothing else you…" He shook his head, and she drew a sharp quick breath of profound relief. "I'm going to need a ride, though—I came in a squad car. I'm sorry to bother you, but is there someone you could ask…?"

"I'll take you. Where do you live?"

"Oh, but you—I'm sure you must be very busy. I don't want—"

"It's no problem. I'm heading back to the shop anyway. Nothing more I can do here." He took a firmer grip on her arm and steered her to the left, away from the media trucks and waiting cameras.

He couldn't have said why he was doing this, not with any truthfulness. He told himself he wanted to ask her some questions, find out more about her and her so-called *impressions.* Never entertained the thought there could be any other reason for spending another minute in the woman's company.

She seems so vulnerable. Is it an act? I'm a cop, I should be able to tell. But I can't. What is it she feels when she looks at me? Does she know about—

But those thoughts he pushed firmly out of his mind and slammed and locked the door to make sure they stayed out.

Okay, so she's one hell of an attractive woman. And I'm a guy. Guys like attractive women, so why should I be any different?

Yeah, but she's not my type, he told himself, kicking that thought out the door, as well. He wasn't exactly sure what his type was, except for one thing: he liked his women sexy and fun and without complications. And while this one could probably pass muster on the first requirement, he had real doubts about the second. And as for number three, well…he was pretty sure *complicated* didn't even begin to describe her.

Neither of them spoke again until they were settled in the front seats of his unmarked gray sedan. She—what was her name? Started with a T. *Terry? Tracy? No—something unusual. Damn.*

"Where to, Miss…" He let it hang just long enough.

"It's Doyle. But please call me Tierney." She glanced at him as she clicked her seat belt into place, and he wondered once more if she'd read his mind and taken pity on him. But she didn't read minds…or claimed she didn't. "Or even Tee," she added, "if you wish. Some people do." Her half smile told him she knew the chances of him doing likewise were slim.

Which was maybe why he said, out of pure contrariness, "Okay, Miss Tee it is, then. I'm Wade, by the way. Wade Callahan." He turned in his seat to offer his hand. Did it out of long habit, then kicked himself for hesitating, for having second thoughts. For wondering whether it was "safe" to touch her, or if physical contact might open up some kind of psychic channel between them. Kicked himself all the more for even thinking those thoughts, knowing it meant he had to believe at least some of what she claimed to be able to do might be real.

Her hand was warm in his, small but vibrant, reminding him of a gentle but wary animal that had allowed him to hold it for one short moment in his grasp.

"Wade," she murmured, and there was a shimmer of amusement in her eyes. Eyes so clear and blue and…yes, *normal,* he wondered how anyone in their right mind could believe she had creepy gifts. The Sight—or whatever she wanted to call it.

He released her hand and was smiling crookedly as he wrapped his around the gearshift lever, wondering whether it was himself or her he was smiling at.

She lived with her grandmother, he discovered, in an apartment above an art gallery called Jeannette's, in a formerly hippieish part of the city that was gradually becoming yuppified. No surprises there; Wade figured if he ever wanted to hang out his psychic shingle it was the place he'd choose. Just enough hippie left to provide plenty of local ambience, with a New Age slant to appeal to the yuppies who went in for that sort of thing.

What did surprise him, though, when Tierney led him through the gallery to the stairs at the back, was how much of the artwork on display actually appealed to him. The watercolors particularly. Not the roses, so much, although he could see the real artistry in them. They were a bit too pretty and feminine—for want of a better word—for his taste. But the waterfalls, now those he wouldn't mind hanging on his own walls. There was something about them… He paused to look closer at one, and a coolness, like fresh moist air, seemed to pour into him, filling all the churning dark places. He felt a strange *easing* inside, a sense of quietude and peace.

"That's Multnomah Falls," Tierney said. "It's one of my favorite places." He hadn't been aware of her coming to stand beside him.

"Yeah," he said, "mine, too." He saw it now, the neat and vaguely archaic signature in the lower righthand corner: *T. Doyle.* He glanced at her and stated the obvious. "These are yours."

She nodded without looking away from the painting, her smile crooked. "When I'm working on a case—like this one—I like to go there, or to places like it. Places where people feel a sense of awe. Or just…happy. Thankful." She nodded at a panel hung with a grouping of the rose paintings. "The Portland Rose Gardens—that's another, and it's closer, easier to get to when I'm…when I need it. Those emotions—good emotions—nourish me. The other kind, the bad emotions…" She shook her head and glanced up at him before moving away. "I don't know why I'm telling you this. I'm sure you're not interested, since you don't believe in what I do."

"Haven't made up my mind on that score, actually." He was surprised to discover that was true, and judging from the smile he glimpsed as he held the door she'd opened, so was she.

He followed her through the door into a small passage-way that led to what appeared to be an office, or maybe a storeroom, and the back entrance to the right, and to the left, a flight of stairs. The space smelled of some sort of cleaning product—maybe several mixed up together. Whatever it was, he couldn't quite place it. "But I'd be interested, whether I believe in what you do or not. I'm always interested in what makes people tick."

"Tick?" A ripple of light laughter drifted down to him as she mounted the stairs ahead of him. "You mean, you'd like to know what my 'racket' is, don't you?"

"Well, sure," he said, carefully screening his enjoyment at the view. "That, too."

On the landing at the top of the stairs, Tierney paused to take a key from the pocket of her slacks and insert it in the door's dead bolt lock.

"If you don't mind waiting here for a moment, I'll see if my grandmother's…" The rest she left hanging as she opened the door and stepped inside, leaving him standing on the landing.

After a moment he pushed on the door she'd left almost closed but unlatched, widening the crack so he could hear what was going on inside the apartment. Didn't hesitate or feel guilty about it, either. That was the thing about being a cop—nosiness pretty much went with the territory.

He heard Tierney call softly, her voice light, sweet, gentle, as if she were talking to a very small child. "Jennie, darling, it's Tee…"

There was a ripple of laughter, low and musical, and a voice to match it said, "Hello, dear."

The next words were muffled, as if by an embrace. "Gran, do you feel like having company? I've brought a friend. His name is Wade Callahan. Would you like to meet him?"

More of that laughter, and the voice took on a certain unmistakable lilt. "Wade Callahan—a fine Irish name! Have him come in, by all means. I'd dearly love to meet him."

"Are you sure? You're not too tired?"

"Not at all, darlin'—what gave you such an idea? I'm never too tired to meet a friend of yours, particularly an Irish lad."

Tierney's face appeared in the partly open doorway, looking flustered. "Sorry about that," she murmured breathlessly as she opened the door wide and beckoned him in. "Detective—ah, Wade, I'd like you to meet my grandmother, Jeannette Doyle."

He didn't know what he'd expected—an invalid, someone frail and ancient, but sprightly, perhaps?—but it sure as hell wasn't the person who rose from a chair near the window as he entered, holding out her hand in greeting.

She was, quite possibly, the most exquisitely beautiful woman he'd ever seen. She wasn't tall, but her slender build and the way she carried herself made her seem so. Her head sat atop her long neck at an angle that made him think of ballerinas in flowing white dresses, or a queen bestowing her grace upon her subjects. Her hands seemed to have a life of their own, like white doves or lilies, and her hair, parted in the middle and falling in gentle waves to her shoulders, was an incredible shade of red-gold that seemed to capture light where there was none and give it back a thousand times brighter. She wore slim black slacks and a long tunic top in a soft sea-green, with iridescent blue-and-gold braided trim around the edges of the draped sleeves and neckline, and open-toed, wedge-heeled gold slippers.

"Wade Callahan, 'tis a pleasure to meet you." Her smile was flirtatious as a girl's, her blue-green eyes bright and wicked.

And it was only then, when she drew near enough to reach out and place those graceful white hands in his, that he saw the lines around her mouth, the softness of her jawline, the fragile crepelike skin around her eyes that gave away her age. Though just what that might be, he wouldn't even venture to guess.

She pulled her hands from his and tilted her head, regarding him in a measuring sort of way. "But you're no more Irish than the pope, now, are you, lad?"

He caught a breath and let it go in a gust of surprised laughter, almost covering Tierney's dismayed gasp.

"Gran!"

"Well, he isn't," the lady hissed back, like an obstinate child.

Tierney shot him a look of mute apology. She seemed tense, watchful, Wade thought, like an anxious parent with a precocious and unpredictable child. His cop sense prickled along the back of his neck, telling him something was "off" here—not dangerous or anything like that—just odd.

"No, it's okay. She's right," he said, surprising himself; his personal history wasn't something he normally shared with strangers. "I was adopted. It's my adoptive parents who are Irish." He smiled winningly at the old lady. "Ma'am, I don't have any idea what I am, to tell you the truth. Mongrel, I expect."

Jeannette hesitated, looked wary, suddenly, and frightened. Wade felt a creeping sensation along the back of his neck as she leaned forward and peered into his face. One frail-looking hand clutched his with surprising strength. "Do I know you?"

"No, Gran," Tierney began, but the old lady had already jerked around to transfer her anxious hands and worried frown to her granddaughter.

"I don't know him, do I? Who is he? What is he doing here? Is he lost?" On that last word, her musical voice dropped to a cracking whisper. "I believe he's lost, Isabella. Go and get him some tea. And some biscuits. He's probably hungry, young boys are always hungry, you know…"

Chapter 2

"Yes, Jennie, darling," Tierney said soothingly as she put her arm around her grandmother's shoulders and gently turned her toward the kitchen, "I'm sure he is hungry. Why don't you go and find some biscuits to go with the tea. And some sandwiches would be nice."

She didn't look at the detective. She was too busy bracing against the fractured emotions—confusion, fear, grief and anger—that radiated from Jeannette in waves at times like these. She couldn't worry right now about what he might be thinking. She'd felt his sharp flash of recognition before the barriers slammed shut like storm shutters, but no doubt the clamor of Jeannette's emotions would have overwhelmed his anyway.

She left her grandmother opening cupboards and muttering to herself and went back to the living room, bracing for the inevitable questions. The suffocating blanket of sympathy.

She found Detective Callahan where she had left him, hands in his pockets, jacket askew, watching her with thoughtful, compassionate eyes.

You're right, Jennie, darling, lost is a better word than missing. He's lost *those pieces of himself.*

"That will occupy her for a while. She won't remember such a complicated task," she explained with a small smile of apology. "She'll sit down at the table and try to pick up the threads, which will be upsetting for her. To avoid it she'll go somewhere inside her mind, somewhere in her past where she was happy. That's where she spends most of her time now."

"Alzheimer's?" the detective asked. She nodded, and he murmured, "I'm sorry." The sympathy was there, but muted, as all his emotions seemed to be.

Except for those bright flashes, like strobe lights in the dark. "So am I. I wish you could have known her the way she was. She was…something."

"She still is."

She threw him a quick, grateful glance and thought, *He has the nicest eyes. Kind eyes.* An instant later she saw those same eyes narrow and become slightly less kind.

"Who is Isabella?"

"You don't miss much, do you?" she said lightly, stepping past him to open the door. "That's my mother's name. Gran calls me that when she's…confused. Which is why I call her Jennie, then—she doesn't understand why I would call her Gran when as far as she's concerned she's my mother."

He followed her onto the landing. "Jennie? Not Mom or Mother?"

"Evidently," she said, without looking up as she closed and locked the door, "that's what my mother called her."

"Evidently?"

"I haven't seen my mother since I was three."

"Ah." His tone was flat, but she felt a wave of something warm, almost like *kinship* wafting after her as he followed her down the stairs. At the bottom he glanced at her before reaching past her to open the door—a gesture of gallantry she suspected must be automatic for him. Someone had taught him manners, and taught them well. "Something we have in common, I guess." She threw him a curious look and he gave her back his wry smile. "I don't remember my mother, either."

She couldn't know what a rare thing it was for him to talk about that stuff—at least he didn't think she could. He sure as hell didn't know what made him do it.

"I never said I don't remember her," she said as she passed him. "My memories of my mother are quite vivid, actually."

"From when you were *three?* Is that part of the…" He waved a hand, trying to think of a term that wouldn't be insulting. "Your psychic thing?"

"In a way, I guess." She smiled at him in a gently forgiving way. "I've gotten all the memories I have of my mother from Jeannette."

It took him maybe three heartbeats to get it. Then he said, "Ah" again—a bit more sardonic, this time. "Your grandmother has it, too, then? This…"

"Gift?" They were passing through the gallery, and he saw Tierney pause to touch the watercolor painting of

Multnomah Falls. He saw tension in the lines between her eyebrows and wondered if she had a headache. "Days like this, it's hard to think of it that way."

Then she seemed to shake it off, whatever the darkness was, and moved on. "My grandmother's...abilities, or whatever you want to call them, are different from mine. I am what is known, in the psychic world—" she cut her eyes at him in a droll way that made him chuckle "—as an *empath*. There's probably a word for what Jeannette is, as well, but I don't know what it is. She just...knows things. About people. Like she knew you aren't really Irish. Plus, she and I have this special connection, I guess, because we can share memories. Normally, I don't really see actual images, but with her I can. Used to, anyway." Her face seemed to cloud over. "I used to see them—her memories of my mother—like photos in an album. Color photos, clear and bright. Now...well, now they're sort of fragmented, like a jumbled jigsaw puzzle."

I have memories like that.

The thought came to him with a flash of surprise, like what his mother used to call a lightbulb moment—from the comics, she'd explain. He heard himself say, "I know what you mean." And frowned, because he hadn't meant to voice the thought out loud.

Tierney glanced up at him, smiling her gentle smile.

Yes...I think you do. That's what these flashes I keep getting from you are all about. We've a kinship, you and I, whether you like it or not. The truth is, neither of us had a chance to know our parents.

"How old were you when you were adopted?" And she wondered, even as she asked it, how she'd found the audacity to probe into the personal business of so guarded and resistant a man.

She was greatly surprised when he hitched a shoulder in an offhand way and answered her. "I don't know—six, I think. Maybe seven."

"Really? You weren't a baby, then. What happened to your parents?" But this time she knew at once she'd gone too far. She saw his jaw tighten, and he didn't answer right away. She muttered, "I'm sorry," putting up a hand as if to stop herself. "Forgive me, please. I'm not— It's none of my business, I know."

The detective let out a breath, frowning. "No, it's a legitimate question, considering the conversation." He paused, shifting his car keys from one hand to the other and back again, then turned to her. "They're dead, that's all I know." His grin appeared, tilted in a way that made curious pleasure-ripples course through her chest. "Believe me, as a police detective it irks me no end to have to admit that. I've tried—" He broke it off with a shake of his head, seemed to hesitate, then turned to the gallery door.

"Do you remember them?" Tierney asked softly. "Your parents?"

She was unprepared for the sudden surge of emotion, followed by a withdrawal so abrupt it was almost violent, like a slap in the face. She stepped back reflexively, and so almost missed his reply, spoken in a quiet voice and without turning.

"I don't remember anything from before I was adopted."

Still reeling from the emotional one-two punch, she couldn't have spoken even if she'd been able to think of what to say. After a brief but electric silence, he threw her a glance that didn't quite make contact.

"Yeah, look—I need to get back to the job."

"Yes," she said. "Of course."

"Let me know if you get any more on our killer—or the victims."

He pushed the door open and went out, hurrying, like someone escaping from a trap.

She wasn't sure why she followed him. But she did. And when she stepped onto the sidewalk, she felt as if she'd collided with an electric fence. Energy sizzled along her scalp and crawled over her body, just beneath her skin. Even her bones seemed to vibrate. As if it were frantically batting at a bombardment of tennis balls, her tired mind tried to give names to the overwhelming emotions ricocheting inside her head.

Watching...watching...

Waited...searched...so long!

Found you!

Glee!

Victory!

Success! At last!

The only thing she knew for certain was that someone was *watching*. Watching with riveted attention and avid interest, a focus so intense it felt like a laser beam. *Watching Wade.*

A few dozen yards down the block, the police detective was getting into his car. She called out to him—a croak, at first, then louder. "Detective Callahan—Wade! Wait—please!"

He turned to look at her across the roof of his car. He was frowning because his heart was beating way faster than it had any reason to, unless he wanted to count having just scared himself silly, coming so close to telling a woman he didn't know or trust things he'd never told another living soul. Right now half of him wanted to ignore her, jump in his car and get the hell out of there, get back to dealing with things he knew were real, and knew what to do with—like facts and evidence and witnesses. Dead bodies. Those things he understood.

Fortunately the other half reminded him that he'd just told this woman to let him know if she picked up anything more on his killer—or his victims. And even if he wasn't sure whether he believed in her "gift," the department had made her part of his team, and it behooved him to listen to what she had to say.

He watched her hurry toward him, breaking into a run the last few yards so that she arrived breathless and pink-cheeked, reminding him once again of a high school cheerleader.

Except, as she came close, he got a good look at her eyes, and against all reason and everything he thought he believed in, his skin began to crawl. He'd seen that look before.

Damn, he wished he didn't have to ask it. But he did. "What is it? Radar pick up something?"

A pained smile flashed on and off like a light with a bad connection. "It was…someone was here, Wade. Just now. I think he's gone, though…"

She didn't look around, as anyone else would have, to see if she could see someone lurking in the vicinity. No— this lady closed her eyes and went still. Looking inside her own head. It gave him cold chills.

"What do you mean, someone was here? This have anything to do with—"

"No—I mean, no, not the case. At least, I don't think

so. But…he was watching *you,* Wade. It was like…he'd been waiting. Looking for you. For a long time. And now he's found you. He was so…happy about it. *Gleeful.*"

Well, hell. What was he supposed to say to that? He ducked his head and ran a hand over the crisp stubble of his short-cropped hair while he thought about it, then lifted it up again when he heard her say softly, "You don't believe me."

She was standing with her arms folded, and he got the impression she was shivering, or trying hard not to. Even though she was on the opposite side of the car from him, he felt a thoroughly ridiculous urge to put his arms around her and warm her. Anything to get her to stop.

"Nah, look, it's not that," he said, trying to smile when what he felt like doing was grinding his teeth. "It's just— look, thanks for the heads-up, okay? You said whoever it was is gone now, right?" She nodded, and he was relieved that her eyes were vivid and focused again. Although he had a feeling the image of those eyes would be staying with him for a while.

"Let me know if he comes back," he said, and he got in his car and headed back downtown.

Pride made him wait until he'd turned the corner before he checked his rearview mirror. Well, hell. He was involved in a murder investigation, after all, and it was a long way from being his first. Not too much of a stretch to think somebody could take a notion to come looking for him with revenge on his mind.

It wasn't much of a stretch, either, for a so-called psychic looking for a way to convince a skeptic to think of that, too.

* * *

Tierney watched the detective's car until it had disappeared around the corner at the end of the block, absently rubbing her arms even though the chill that always followed an *impression* had already faded. She turned and went back into the gallery, frowning uneasily and wondering whether she'd done the wrong thing, telling Detective Callahan about the entity she already thought of as The Watcher. He was already teetering on the edge of disbelief, and passing along an *impression* so vague and meaningless was bound to only increase his skepticism. Especially since she hadn't gotten any sense that The Watcher meant any harm.

The Watcher. From the objectivity of ten minutes removed from the experience, she replayed that extrasensory bombardment over again in her mind, searching for any signs of malevolence or danger. She couldn't recall anything negative in it at all—quite the opposite, in fact. She kept getting that overwhelming sense of success achieved after great effort. Triumph. Intense glee. Profound relief. *Joy.*

What it reminded her of, she realized, was an image from a television miniseries she'd seen years ago, about a black American man searching for his roots in Africa. She'd never forgotten the look on the man's face—an actor, of course, but no less emotionally intense, at least for her— when he heard at last the old griot, the verbal historian, recount the familiar story of how his ancestor had been taken by slavers. The man's incredible, overwhelming joy as he cried out, *"I've found you, you old African! I've found you!"*

Yes. It was that kind of feeling. So vivid it shook her,

brought tears to her eyes and goose bumps to her skin even now.

Laughing at herself, she dashed the tears from her eyes, rubbed away the goose bumps and went back into the gallery. She walked slowly among the paintings, soaking in their sunlit freshness and tranquility one last time before climbing the stairs to her apartment…and the darkness that was Jeannette.

Ed Francks was on the phone when Wade walked into the squad room. He covered the mouthpiece with his hand and muttered, "See the boss," as he jerked his head in the general direction of the hallway that dog-legged off the main squad room.

Wade nodded, tossed his jacket over the back of his chair and tucked in his shirttails as he headed for the office of the homicide division chief. It was more automatic than necessary; the current chief wasn't a stickler for spit and polish. The only thing that impressed Nola Hoffman was closing cases.

Nola, being five-ten and a little bit—six feet in the high-heeled pumps she always wore—and carrying more weight than she probably wanted to, was more than impressive enough to fit her title. It didn't hurt, either, that she had skin the exact color of Hershey's milk chocolate, a neck about a foot long topped off with a perfectly shaped head that was covered with maybe half an inch of fuzz the color of vanilla ice cream and the face of an Egyptian pharaoh. She was referred to as "Boss" to distinguish her from the head of Special Cases, Allan Styles, who was just about Nola's direct opposite in every way. Styles was known as "The

Chief" to his face; what most of Wade's fellow homicide cops called him behind his back was considerably less respectful and a whole lot more colorful. Dwight Cutter, Chief of Police of the City of Portland, was never called anything but "Chief Cutter," both to his face and behind his back.

Under the circumstances, Wade wasn't surprised to find all three of those individuals gathered in the Homicide Division chief's office, their faces turned expectantly toward him as he entered. The only wonder to him was that his honor the mayor hadn't chosen to join them, as well.

"Chief Cutter… Chief Styles… Boss…" Wade said as handshakes and nods were exchanged and appropriate titles acknowledged all around. He then assumed parade-rest stance, since all available chairs in the office had been taken, and arranged his features in an expression he hoped would appear both alert and somber.

"I've just been telling Chief Cutter and Chief Styles about our task force," Nola said, leaning forward to place both forearms on her desk, the center part of which had, in their honor, been swept clean of papers clear down to the blotter. "Detective, can you fill us in on the latest developments?"

Wade managed to get his throat cleared, but Chief Cutter beat him to the actual forming of words. "Understand we had another torture murder last night. What's this make now, five?"

"Five with roughly the same M.O., yes, sir. Assuming they're all connected. We haven't established that they are, not for certain."

Styles, who'd never been Wade's biggest fan, said with a superior smirk, "Come on, Callahan, all five victims have been—"

But Cutter's blunt "Why not?" overrode it.

Wade chose to respond to the chief of police. "There's no connection between the victims, for one thing. Except gender—all were female. Age-wise, we have a college student, a retiree, a city bus driver and a middle-aged housewife. Now this new one—she's a widow, three grown kids. All were tortured in approximately the same way. None was sexually assaulted, although they were left naked and hanging by their wrists, and no clothes or IDs have been found."

"But you have positive IDs on the victims?"

"Yes, sir—missing persons matchups and next-of-kin verification on the first four. The most recent—our widowed mom—had fingerprints on file. Seems she was a docent at the art museum."

"No suspects, I take it."

"No, sir. So far, there's been no physical evidence left at the crime scenes by the killer or killers. None of the victims had any enemies, owed anybody money, took drugs or fooled around with anyone's husband, girl or boyfriend. Model citizens, all."

"Hell, sounds like we got ourselves a serial killer to me." Chief Cutter snorted, fixing his jowly features in a Churchillian scowl. "Looks like I get the honor of breaking the news to the mayor. Just what this city needs—another serial killer. We got the Rose Festival coming up in a couple weeks, the eyes of the country on us—in a good way, for a change. How long's it been since the last time we had a serial killer? Fifteen years? Back in the nineties, wasn't it?"

"It's spring," Styles said. "Warm weather always brings out the weirdos."

"Weirdos we got plenty of—always have. Wouldn't be Portland without 'em. At least they're not generally homicidal, thank the Lord." Cutter pushed himself to his feet. Once at eye level with Wade—and with an unmistakable gleam in his eye—the police chief said, "Speaking of weirdos, how's the newest member of your team working out, Detective?"

Nobody made the mistake of taking that question at face value. Everyone in the room was familiar with Chief Cutter's habit of setting conversational traps for unwary subordinates, and well aware of from whence the order to involve the psychic had originated.

So it was that Wade addressed an audience perhaps more respectfully attentive than it might otherwise have been. "Ah...well, sir, so far she seems..." He coughed, hoping to gain time for his brain to find a word that wouldn't get him in trouble with his boss and make him the butt of department humor for the foreseeable future. When the word failed to appear, he started again. "From the crime scene this morning, she did pick up that the, uh, latest victim didn't know her killer." He paused while everyone nodded gravely, then continued with an absolutely straight face. "Oh, yeah—and the killer doesn't like uniforms."

There was a snuffle of poorly stifled laughter from someone—probably Styles. Nola put one long-boned hand over the lower part of her face and became suddenly interested in a large spill of something on her desk blotter.

Chief Cutter pushed abruptly to his feet and favored each person in the room individually with two seconds of jaw-jutting scowl. If it hadn't been for the city-wide smoking ban, Wade knew, there would have been a cigar clamped between his teeth. "I expect everyone in this department to give the gal some time. She's done a good job for other departments, and Lord knows this one, and this city needs all the help it can get." He took a step toward the door, then jerked around to stab two fingers—holding the invisible cigar between them, of course—at the room in general. "I don't need to tell you, we need this sicko caught. I want this thing wrapped up before the Rose Festival begins. That clear?"

Amid three mumbled *Yes, sirs,* the chief of police made his exit.

Tee placed the bowl of thick chicken-and-barley soup in front of her grandmother and the spoon alongside it, then unfolded a dish towel and draped it over her grandmother's lap. "There you are, Jennie, just the way you like it."

Jeannette, thankfully in one of her sweet moods, smiled up at her. "That's very kind of you, dear. Such a lovely lass…my, but you remind me of my daughter. Her name is…" A look of stark distress wiped away her smile.

"Isabella," Tee said quickly, before the distress could blossom into panic.

The old lady's face brightened, although her eyes remained vague…unfocused. "Oh—you know my daughter? Are you one of her little friends? I used to know all her friends. Boyfriends, too. She always has boyfriends, my Isabella. Well, she's such a pretty thing, 'tis no wonder…"

Tee picked up the spoon and gently curled her grandmother's fingers around it. "Here, Jennie, dear, try the soup. It's barley—you like barley."

Jeannette obediently dug into the soup bowl and slurped

a noisy spoonful, making humming sounds of approval as she worked it around in her mouth. She swallowed, then gave a trill of musical laughter. It sounded poignantly young. "Izzy always brings her young men home to meet me, you know. She hasn't The Gift herself—doesn't like mine much, either, except when it suits her. Like when she wants to know what's in a boy's heart. *Then* she doesn't mind it, not a bit…" She scooped up another bite of soup, still chuckling to herself.

Tee leaned her chin on her hand as she watched her grandmother attack the bowl of soup with gusto, crooning and mumbling to it as she ate. "I wish you could help me know what's in this one's heart, because I sure can't," she said, knowing Jeannette wouldn't really hear her, that she was years away, now. A lifetime away.

"Wade Callahan…that's his name—the detective I'm working with now. You said he's lost, Jennie, and I think he is, but only parts of him. He's like…a jigsaw puzzle with pieces missing." She sighed. "I can't read him."

Jeannette paused with the spoon on its downward arc. "I could never read my Tommy, either."

"Tommy?" Tee felt excitement vibrate through her breastbone. Her grandmother's voice had taken on a different timbre…a younger, lighter pitch, with a definite Irish brogue. Softly she asked, "Was he your boyfriend, Jennie?"

"Boyfriend? Oh, well, I s'pose he was to begin with, before I married him." She chuckled. "Tommy was my husband, of course."

Tee felt her grandmother's emotions fill her head, warm and sweet, at first, like spring breezes wafting through orchards of apple trees. Then just as quickly they changed to hot, sultry winds, blowing gusts that smelled of passion and storms.

"I never knew you were married," she said in a wondering voice. She'd always assumed single parenthood was the norm in her family.

"Not for long, I'm afraid," Jeannette said in the gently wistful manner of one reliving an old, old tragedy. "My Tommy was killed, you see, only weeks after we married, when I was already carrying his daughter. My lovely Isabella—looked just like him, she did, and took after him in other ways, as well. Reckless, he was. Always takin' risks. Went off to Belfast to fight the British. And I couldna' stop it…" Her accent seemed to thicken as a tear trickled down her cheek. "I saw. I did. But I wouldna' believe."

Tee couldn't answer. One hand covered her mouth; the other groped blindly for her grandmother's as waves of inconsolable grief washed over her.

Later, after the effects of the *impression* had faded, she remembered the words. *I saw, but I wouldna' believe.*

And felt a chill of an altogether different kind.

In a motel room on the outskirts of Portland, a private investigator named Holt Kincaid took out his cell phone and punched a number on his speed dial. A woman answered, a voice he knew well. It sounded sleepy.

"Hey, Sam," he said with momentary qualms of guilt, "did I wake you?"

"Hey, Holt," his employer's wife muttered in her mild Georgia drawl. "'S okay. What's up?"

"Sorry—keep forgetting about the time difference. It's pretty late there, right?"

"Yeah, but never mind, I'm up now." Her voice sounded less grumpy and more alert, so he figured she hadn't missed the burr of excitement in his. "So, give. You wouldn't be calling this late if you hadn't found something."

"Uh, is Cory around? He ought to be the first one to hear this."

"He's on assignment. He'll be checking in, though, so tell me. And, Holt?"

"Yeah."

"If you don't spill it to me this minute, I swear I will send a very large, very muscular—"

"Okay, okay. I've found something, all right. Not some-*thing,* actually—some*one.*" He paused, surprised to find a constriction in his throat. Damn, but this case had gotten personal. Too personal. He coughed and said, "It's…Wade. I've found Wade."

There was silence, then a rustling sound, as if his listener had sat down rather abruptly. The voice, barely audible, said, "You…found him? You're sure? Honest to—"

"Swear to God." Holt couldn't hold back elated laughter. "His name's Callahan, and he's a cop—yeah, just like Dirty Harry. A homicide detective in Portland, Oregon."

"Have you talked to him? Does he…"

"No. I've been watching him for a couple days—just wanted to be sure before I called you guys. I figured Cory should be the one to…you know, break the news."

"Yeah." There was a long exhalation, then a whispered, "My God. I can't believe you found him. It's been so long—I was beginning to think—"

"Yeah," said Holt, "me, too. But this is bound to lead to the others. Wade and the other boy—"

"Matthew."

"Right. They were adopted by the same couple. I figure he's got to know where his brother is."

"Oh, Holt—this is beyond great. It's...it's... Oh, man, I can't wait to tell Cory. We're going to find them all, I just know it." Holt wasn't sure, but he thought he heard a break in Sam's voice before she added, "The little girls, too."

"They're not little girls anymore," he said gruffly. "They're a couple of grown-up women, now. And they were just babies when it all went down. They're not going to remember."

"I know. But still." Holt heard a sniff. Unmistakable, this time.

"Sammie June, darlin', are you crying? *Samantha?* Tough-as-nails charter pilot, never let 'em see you—"

There was a quiet click in his ear and the cell phone went dead.

The ringing telephone woke Tee from a restless early morning slumber. Sweaty and achy, she threw back the tumbled covers and stretched her back, trying to work out some of the stiffness resulting from a poor night's sleep before picking up the phone. Which, by that time, had activated the answering machine. She listened, yawning, to her embarrassingly chirpy outgoing message, then stiffened, suddenly wide awake, when she heard the impatient voice begin its reply.

She snatched it up, shaking and jangled from a burst of adrenaline. "Wade—Detective Callahan—yes, I'm here. What is—"

The detective's voice was terse. Flat. "Sorry to wake you. We've got another one."

"Oh—God…"

"And, Miss Doyle?"

"Tee—please."

"Okay, Miss *Tee.* What you said about our killer not liking uniforms? Well, looks like he was serious about that, because he just killed a cop. She was one of ours."

Chapter 3

Wade stomped the brake, jerked the car to a stop and slapped the gearshift lever into Park. The violence seemed the only way his body would operate, with anger spraying like shrapnel through every nerve.

"Bastard left her hanging from a chain-link fence," he said, spitting out the words in bitter bites. "Left her hanging there like a broken doll." That's what she'd looked like—a little broken doll.

He opened the door and got out, then paused with one hand on the roof of the car to look back at his passenger, sitting silent and motionless with her seat belt still fastened. "You coming?"

She looked up at him like someone awakened from a doze, then nodded. He noticed that she was deathly pale;

her freckles reminded him of dried blood speckles on white paper. Her hand shook as she unbuckled her seat belt.

He looked across the roof of the car at the gray industrial landscape—slabs of concrete and asphalt broken by blocks of corrugated tin buildings and zigzags of chain-link fencing, the only color provided by the yellow or green of a forklift or skid loader tractor, and the flashing lights of the law enforcement and crime scene vehicles gathered like buzzards around a fresh kill. Grim enough on a sunny day, let alone like it was now, socked in by the early morning fog.

Helluva place for a young woman to leave this earth. Helluva way for a cop to die.

But just the same, he felt like crap for letting his anger loose the way he'd been doing. Should've remembered the woman—okay, Tierney, Miss *Tee,* psychic or empath or whatever she was—picked up on emotions. Clearly she'd picked up on his, and the toll it had taken on her couldn't have been faked.

He took a deep breath, then ducked his head back inside the car to say gruffly, "It's okay, you know, if you want to take a minute."

She reached for the door handle. "No, that's okay. I'm fine."

She opened her door and he slammed his and went around the car to take her arm, which he figured was the least he could do. She didn't object, although she probably didn't need his help. Her step was steady enough and she kept pace with him easily as they hurried across the broken asphalt, weaving between the jumble of department vehicles that had circled the crime scene like covered wagons in order to screen from curious eyes what to them was a personal tragedy.

He wondered if she felt the same weird tingle he did where his fingers touched her.

Thank God, at least they'd got the body down off the fence and decently covered. Crime scene be damned, she was a police officer. No way in hell they'd leave her hanging there, naked and desecrated like that. *Alicia.* Her name was Alicia. Wade knew her slightly, had gone through the academy with her. Seemed like he recalled something about her getting engaged recently. Her fiancé was in the service. In Iraq.

"Damn."

He didn't realize he'd spoken out loud until Tierney paused and looked at him. "Sorry," he muttered. "I'm just…"

"You're not the only one." Her lips had a pinched look, her eyes squinted as if she had a fearsome headache. "There's so much anger here. So much rage. I can't pick up anything else. From the killer or…"

"Damn," he said again, and this time exhaled with frustration. Again, he hadn't thought about the effects of so much emotional fallout on the crime scene. *Her* crime scene. It must be the equivalent of a thunderstorm blowing through his. "Would it help if I had everyone clear out? Leave you alone with…" He couldn't bring himself to say "the body."

A smile flicked briefly at her lips. "Too late—it's already been contaminated." As if she'd read his thought.

Then, looking uncertain, she paused, turned to him and said, "Maybe, if I…"

"What?"

"If I looked at her." Her blue eyes clung to his, stark with fear.

He felt something in his chest contract. Ignoring that, and squelching whatever sympathy he felt for her, or admiration for her courage, he said gruffly, "Are you sure you want to do that?" He couldn't afford the sympathy, damn it. A cop was dead. He wanted to catch this dirtbag—whatever it took.

After a long moment she nodded. He saw her throat move as she swallowed.

"All right, then." He reached out to her, touched her shoulder. Then, taking her once more by the arm, he guided her through the busy hive of crime scene techs and law enforcement officers, some in uniform, some not. When he drew near to the cadre of officers standing guard around the gurney and the small, shrouded form that lay on it, he spoke to them in a low voice that was mindful of their taut, angry faces and grief-filled eyes. "Gonna ask you to step back for a few minutes, if you would, please." The line shifted, and drew in more tightly around the gurney. "Come on, guys, give us a minute, okay? Give this lady some room."

Finally, with nods and murmurs and shufflings, the line broke, then moved reluctantly back, opening a passage to admit the stranger, the civilian. The outsider.

Wade drew Tierney gently forward and positioned her beside the body, then knelt and drew back the sheet just far enough to uncover the victim's face.

Someone had closed her eyes, he saw. But no way in hell did she look like she was sleeping. Her skin, he remembered, had been a rich warm shade of brown. Now it was a muddy gray, blotched with traces of tears and speckled with her own blood.

Steeling himself, he sat back on his haunches, pivoted and looked up at Tierney, who was standing frozen, staring down at the ravaged face. As he watched, her own drained of all color and her eyes went wide with shock and horror.

Well, *hell*. Okay, he'd pretty much expected that. What he didn't expect was when she then uttered a small, muffled cry, turned and pushed her way through the line of cops, and once free of the crowd, broke into a desperate, stumbling run.

Swearing to himself and muttering apologies to his fellow officers, Wade went after her.

He found her behind the CSI van, leaning one shoulder against it and looking as if her knees were about to buckle. She had one hand over her mouth and the other arm folded across her stomach, but even though she had her back to him he knew instantly she wasn't sick, as he'd supposed, but crying. He could see her shoulders shaking, hear the sobbing sounds she made even though she tried to muffle them with her hand.

He knew she was having a moment of pure panic, though only God knew why. He was accustomed to handling crying women; in his line of work he encountered more than his share of them. They just seemed to naturally gravitate to him. He'd taken some ribbing around the squad room, and earned the nickname "Papa Bear" because of it, too. He didn't like to think about why this particular woman's tears affected him differently. Why they made him hurt deep down in his chest. Why they made his belly quiver.

He hesitated, part of him wanting to turn tail and walk away and leave her there with her privacy and her grief. Lord knows he didn't need this, not now.

But then she turned and looked at him with her flooded

cheeks and anguished eyes, and no surprise whatsoever. And he kicked himself for once again forgetting who and what she was. Of course she'd know he was there.

"I saw her," she said, and her voice was choked and thick. "Yesterday...when I—the uniforms. What I said about him—the k-killer. About hating uniforms. I didn't understand. It was *her.* He'd already chosen—if I'd only—"

He didn't remember moving, but somehow his arms were wrapped around her, holding her close, and the rest of her litany of blame was muffled by his chest. He felt his heart thumping against her cheek, and he cradled her head in his hand and nestled it more comfortably there.

"You couldn't have stopped it," he said, the words low and gruff and blown through her hair in soft puffs. "Even if you'd known what you were seeing. Feeling. Hey—we're gonna get this guy. It was too late for her, and that's not on you. But we *will* get him—I promise you. Okay? We will get him."

After a moment Tierney nodded and whispered, "Okay."

She should have pulled away then. Should have stepped back, put a discreet distance between herself and the safe and peaceful harbor of the police detective's arms. But for some reason she couldn't make herself move. She wasn't normally a toucher—didn't really like to *be* touched, either, especially by strangers. Touching someone, she'd found, opened too broad a channel to the emotions, often exposed even those emotions people kept buried, but shallowly, just under the facades they presented to the world. But here, enfolded in this man's arms, she felt only peace. A wondrous, restful *stillness.* As if the barricades he'd built to block his own emotions kept all others from intruding, as well. After the bombardment she'd just endured, the respite was almost too lovely to bear.

"Uh, Lieutenant— Oh, sorry…"

Just that easily the peace was shattered.

Tierney stiffened, and so did the arms that sheltered her. She moved away from her protector, wiping hastily at her cheeks, while he turned, frowning, to meet the intruder. She'd met him before—a tough-looking, middle-aged black man with kind eyes. She could feel concern and compassion rolling off of him in gentle waves, flowing over her like healing oil.

"Yeah, Ed," Wade said.

The black man's eyes slipped past him to find Tierney instead. "You doin' okay, ma'am?"

"She's fine. What've you got?"

"Crime scenes can be tough, I know." He was still looking at Tierney. "I believe I'd worry if you didn't feel bad."

She nodded. Wade made a growling sound low in his throat and the other cop turned his attention back to him without undue haste.

"Yeah, partner…got something over here I think you're gonna want to see."

The two men started off at a hurrying pace, and since no one told her she shouldn't, Tierney followed. The truth was, she felt a little ashamed about losing control the way she had, and was hoping for a chance to redeem herself.

Wade followed his former partner past the crime scene and the knot of official vehicles and into the maze of industrial buildings and loading docks that ran along the riverfront. He turned into a long, wide avenue that ran between two rows of buildings, bisected by a drainage channel and lined with trash bins, where several CSIs were busily setting out numbered markers and taking photographs. The primary object of their interest appeared to be a small pile of ashes and charred fabric located in the drainage channel about halfway down the row.

"Couple of unis found it during a routine canvas of the area," Ed said. "Ashes were still warm and wet, so that puts the time about right."

"What makes you think it isn't just some wino's campfire?"

"This." Ed looked at the CSI hovering near the pile.

She nodded, and with a pair of tweezers carefully picked up a tiny scrap of partly charred fabric that had been marked with a numbered flag. She held it so Wade could get a close look at it. He did, and felt his stomach go cold. Small as it was, it was instantly recognizable as a piece of the Portland P.D. uniform's shoulder patch.

The CSI put the scrap back where she'd found it and stepped back to give him room. He squatted down to get a closer look, and that was when the smell hit him.

"Whoa," he said, rearing back, "tell me that's not—"

Ed snorted. "Yeah, it is. The dirtbag peed on it."

"It was the final insult."

Three heads jerked toward the new voice. Tierney was standing a few yards away, arms folded across her waist, so quietly they'd all but forgotten she was there. Her face had that pale, pinched look again, but this time she seemed to have herself in better control.

"It's the uniform he despises," she went on in the same uneven, almost-gentle voice. "Particularly women in uniform. He tortures them while they're wearing the uniform, then strips it off before he kills them. To make them see they're weak without it—that they're nothing at all, not even human. They can't hurt him. But in his mind the uniform is the source of power. It *can* hurt him. So he has to 'kill' it, too. He burns it. And when it's nothing but ashes, he...um—"

"Urinates on it," Wade said grimly. "As you said, it's the final act of desecration." She nodded. He looked at her for a long moment, and in her shimmering eyes he saw what it must have cost her to feel what she'd felt, and speak of it so calmly.

He rose and nodded to the CSI, who went back to methodically measuring and photographing and cataloging while he took Tierney's arm and turned her away from the pitiful remains of Officer Alicia Williams's uniform.

"There's nothing more we can do here," he said in a hard voice as Ed fell into step with him. "Just let the techs and science people do their jobs. We need to move on this uniform angle. And *fast*. The bastard's killed twice in two days. What I want to know is, why didn't we find his burn site at the other crime scenes?"

Ed shrugged. "Didn't canvas wide enough? Maybe he had to go a ways to find a safe place. Here, he had this whole complex pretty much to himself. And maybe the other vics weren't wearing the uniform when they were killed, who knows?"

"They were," Tierney said, the rapid pace making her voice bumpy. "It's part of what makes him...I don't know what you call it—"

"It's the trigger," Wade said grimly. "Ed, get back to the squad. I want everybody available looking for some kind of uniform link for the other vics."

"The last one was a docent at the art museum," Ed reminded him. "Don't they wear uniforms?"

Wade nodded. "That's two. Work the others. If you find a connection, then start working on a profile for our killer. I'm thinking we're looking at a victim of abuse, here. Most likely at the hands of a woman. A woman in uniform. Could be his mother, could be—"

"It's not his mother," Tierney said, then threw him a look of apology. "At least, I don't think so. I don't get that kind of feeling from him. I think it may have been some kind of institution. A school…or an orphanage…"

"I don't think they even have orphanages anymore, do they?" Ed said doubtfully.

"I don't know," Wade said, "but we need to find out."

"If you're still thinking you could have done anything to prevent this latest killing, you need to quit," Wade growled after they'd driven half of the way back to Tierney's apartment in silence.

Tierney stirred and looked over at him. "I'm not."

"It was a good lead. Now we know what the victims have in common—at least the last two, and I'm going out on a limb, here, and saying odds are the others will, too. We know what the trigger is. We're beginning to know who we're dealing with and how we might be able to start looking for him. That's huge."

She gave a small sigh. "I was just thinking about…him. Who he is, what made him what he is."

She didn't tell the hard-edged cop she was beginning to feel some sympathy for the man she knew he must think of as a vicious animal. It was one of the hazards of being an empath, and she'd learned to keep those feelings to herself. But she understood now that the person they were trying so desperately to find was a victim himself, that like so many who are driven to kill, he'd been shaped—warped—by unspeakable cruelty at the hands of someone who should have been his protector.

"So," said Wade, "let's hear it."

She looked away, smiling. "You're asking me to be a profiler?"

He hitched one shoulder. "Why not? I have an idea a lot of profilers—the best ones, anyway—probably have some of what you've got. Empathy—the ability to get inside a person's skin. Seems to me it's just a question of to what degree." When she didn't reply but went on smiling, he looked over at her and said, *"What?"*

"I guess…I'm surprised. I didn't think you were a believer."

She could see the side of his mouth tilted in a grin. "You mean, I can surprise you? I thought you could read me like a book."

She gave a soft huff of laughter. "I'm sure you find that idea distressing, to say the least. May I remind you, I don't read thoughts. Only emotions. And the truth is, you know, you can block me—and you do. Most people can—and do. Not just from me, from everyone. Sometimes consciously, sometimes unconsciously, but for sure if they know someone like me is tuning in. The reason I can pick up so much from crime scenes is because, for one thing, it's after the fact. The emotions were broadcast at a time when no one was around, so there wasn't any need to block them. And, of course, the emotions are so powerful, so…" *Awful. Horrible. Ugly. Violent.*

"Yeah," said Wade, as if he'd heard her. He frowned.

"What I don't get, I guess, is how you can pick up these emotions 'after the fact,' as you put it. That's where I part company with believing."

"I'm not sure myself, actually. I don't think there's ever been a scientific study done. I have my own theory, if you care to hear it. As you might imagine, it's a question I get asked a lot."

"Sure, I want to hear it."

She paused, took a preparing breath. "Okay, think about the way you pick up scents...odors. What you're picking up is actually molecules of a substance that are suspended in the air. You take them in along with the air you breathe, your scent receptors pass them along to your brain, which identifies them for you."

"Lovely thought," Wade said dryly, "considering the things I get to smell on a regular basis."

She gave him a sympathetic smile before continuing. "Okay, then there are sound waves. You can't see them, but they travel through the air, your ears pick them up, and all the little thingies inside there do their job and the sounds get transmitted to your brain, which once again identifies them, based on the database of all your stored-up experiences. Now, it's pretty much recognized that thoughts are a form of energy—like electricity. Or maybe it *is* a form of electricity—I'm not sure. But that energy can travel, and it can remain suspended in the air, and no one knows the limits of how far or for how long. And it can be picked up by someone who's sensitive enough to recognize it."

"People like you."

"Yes," Tierney said, turning to look at him, "but sometimes the sensitivity comes from having a very close relationship. You've heard stories about mothers who somehow *know* when their child is hurt, or in danger, no matter how far away they are."

"Yeah, or you think the phone's going to ring, and then it does." Wade snorted. "What about all the times you think the phone's going to ring and it doesn't? Just the law of averages says you're bound to hit it once in a while."

"True." She let it go at that. She knew from long experience the pointlessness of this discussion.

After a moment Wade said, "So, what about that profile? We are dealing with a male, right?"

"Absolutely."

"Someone who was abused, probably by a woman—not his mother—wearing a uniform. Right so far?"

"Yes…" She frowned, reluctant to sort through those impressions again, but knowing she must. Bracing herself firmly, she closed her eyes and opened her memory. "He's young, I think—no more than thirty-five. A loner. Parents…dead, I think. Anyway, haven't been around for a long time."

"He's probably been in the system, then," Wade said, nodding. "We'll check that out. What else?"

"He's shy, timid, even. A mouse, afraid of people. Feels threatened by them, especially women. Feels powerless. Probably works at a menial job—whatever it is, he hates it. He fantasizes about—" She couldn't go on. Slammed the door shut with a shudder of revulsion.

"Yeah…it's okay." He sounded distracted. Thoughtful.

"What are you thinking?"

He jerked a look at her, then smiled. "Oh, I think you know."

"I don't need to have a gift to know you must be thinking about your own childhood. Losing your parents at an early age. Going into 'the system.'"

His smile vanished completely, then returned, though a little crooked now. "Yeah, but I wasn't abused. I was one of the lucky ones, I guess. My brother and I both."

"You have a brother?" she asked, looking at him with new interest. As a child she'd yearned for brothers and sisters. "How lucky you are."

"Yeah." But his voice held a soft irony, and she felt wisps of emotion leaking through his barriers. An aura of sadness.

She wouldn't normally have pressed, but for some reason she couldn't bear to leave him with the melancholy she'd unwittingly stirred in him. "You seem sad," she said gently. "Were the two of you...not close?"

"Oh, we're close," he said dryly. "At least we were growing up. Stayed that way until pretty recently, too, even though as adults we both went in different directions. We're completely different, when you get right down to it. Guess it's a miracle we got along as well as we did."

"He was younger than you."

He nodded, seemingly not surprised she hadn't made it a question. "Matt always was kind of a free spirit, I guess you could say—not one for the discipline of a nine-to-five job, anyway. He barely made it through college, and afterward went off to California to explore the great outdoors. Wound up staying there. He was doing okay, working as a wilderness guide—rock climbing, white-water river rafting, that sort of thing."

"What happened?"

He let out a breath and she winced involuntarily as the sadness became sharp, almost too painful to bear. He looked at her and muttered, "Oh—sorry," and instantly she felt the pain being dampened down, covered with wrappings, brought once again under control.

"He had an accident," he said in his flat, policeman's voice. "Rock climbing. Broke his back. He's paralyzed from the waist down."

"Oh, how awful," Tierney murmured, knowing how inadequate it was, pressing her fingers against the spot at the base of her throat that ached with the pressure of his sadness.

"Yeah." After a long pause he went on. "So anyway, he kind of…dropped out. Last I heard he was down in L.A.— works at a sports center, something like that. He does wheelchair sports, I know that, but he doesn't keep in very close touch nowadays."

"What about your parents? Do you keep in touch with them? Does he?"

"About Matt, I couldn't tell you. I try to keep in touch. We talk on the phone every couple of weeks. They live in Florida. My mom says she'd rather have hurricanes than earthquakes and volcanoes—says at least with hurricanes you get some warning." He made an exasperated sound, but one with affection in it.

Silence fell. They were coming into Tierney's neighborhood. In a few more minutes she'd be home. Home alone with only her painting and the sad remnants of Jeannette, the only family she had left, to keep the terrible emotion-memories at bay. Frustration and anger swept over her— her own emotions for a change. Memories of the peace she'd known when Wade had held her only made her anguish worse.

Why can't I have that always? Someone of my own, someone for me, *someone to care for me and nurture me and protect me from the bad stuff?*

They stopped at a traffic light. She looked at Wade's stalwart profile, resenting him a little bit then, for being stalwart, yes, but also for being oblivious to *her* emotions. Knowing she was being unfair. Irrational. But still…

"Wade," she said, "do you think about them—your birth parents? Do you remember them at all?"

He looked over at her, then back up at the light. Seconds passed, and she thought he wouldn't answer her. And then he did—with a lie.

"Nope. Not a thing."

But they tumbled into her mind like broken toys from an overstuffed closet, bits and pieces of emotions and memories, impressions that could only have come from the man sitting placidly beside her, waiting for the light to change. Shards of violence, strangling cobwebs of terror.

He hadn't blocked them. Were they too powerful to contain, or had he simply forgotten? Did that mean he was beginning, even unconsciously, to trust her a little? For a few moments the pleasure that thought stirred in her eclipsed the fact that he'd lied.

The light changed and the car moved forward. Tierney let that sweet, soft breeze of unexpected happiness warm her until the next signal stopped them once more. Then she said, without looking at him, "Don't you think that's odd?"

Wade glanced at her. "What, you mean that I don't remember my birth parents?"

"You said you were six or seven when you lost them. Most people have memories, bits and pieces, at least, from much earlier than that."

He hitched one shoulder. "Well, I don't. If that's odd, I guess I am."

But again the shrapnel of violence and fear screamed into her head, making her wince in spite of her effort not to.

He threw her another look, this one sharp and accompanied by a snort and a sardonic little smile. "I'm guessing you're picking up something. So? Come on, give. I can't wait to hear this."

She shook her head, looked up at the light and said flatly, "It's green."

A polite beep from someone's horn seconded the reminder, and the car jerked forward. They drove for two blocks in total silence before Tierney spoke again, in the same toneless voice. "You missed it."

"What?"

"That was my place back there. Where I live. You missed it."

Swearing, Wade flipped on the blinker and made a screeching right at the next corner. Once again silence reigned inside the car while he maneuvered around the block and into a parking space two doors from Jeannette's Gallery. He turned off the motor but continued to sit facing front, fingers flexing on the steering wheel. Tierney made no move to get out of the car, and neither did he.

Then he thought, *What the hell am I doing?*

Acting like a damn jerk, was what he was doing. And it wasn't him, the sarcasm, the mockery. He didn't like the idea of someone reading him—who would? But it wasn't as if she did it on purpose. And if she had picked up something from his thoughts—emotions, or whatever—so what? Far as he knew, he hadn't been thinking or feeling anything out of line. What was he afraid of?

He let out a breath, a wordless surrender. "Look, that was uncalled for. I'm sorry."

"I know."

He threw her a look in time to catch the remains of a smile, then gave a snort of laughter and ran a hand over his hair. "This is going to take some getting used to. And what happened to my being able to block you?"

She looked back at him with somber eyes. "I don't know. Maybe you let your guard down. Or maybe—"

"What?" he prompted when her gaze slipped away. He caught her arm and she brought her eyes reluctantly back to his. "Come on, what the hell did you see?"

"Feel."

"Whatever."

"It was bits and pieces—like a jigsaw puzzle all mixed up, so a lot of it didn't make sense. But I felt fear. A small child's fear—*terror,* actually. It was powerful."

She paused, and he gave her a shake. Not even aware that he did. "Go on."

"I felt…violence. Trauma. Really awful…" Her voice broke and her eyes darkened, as if the violence she spoke of was reflected in them. Relentless, he was about to prompt her again when she caught a breath and went on. "But there's something else, too. Something else I—*you*—felt. Or remembered. Something changed. You felt *comforted.* The fear was still there, but it was less now, because someone, or something, came between you and the violence. You felt…sheltered. Protected." She gazed at him, now with uncertainty in her eyes. "Maybe…could that have been your parents? Does this mean anything to you?"

He shook his head. Became aware of the way he was gripping her arm and released her. Faced front again and groped blindly for the ignition key. He was all but vibrating with the strain of keeping himself and his thoughts and feelings blocked.

"Not a thing," he said as the engine roared to life.

Tierney nodded without comment, though he knew she didn't believe him. After several tension-filled moments, she opened her door. "Well. Anyway. Thanks for the ride home."

"No problem. I'll, uh…I'll call you if anything develops. And by the way—good job today." She paused to give him a long look, and he felt compelled to add, "Really. You helped a lot."

She nodded, murmured, "Thanks," and closed the door.

He pulled out of the parking space and drove off with as much decorum as he could muster, considering how jangled he was, rather like a normally law-abiding citizen who'd just been ticketed for a traffic violation. He was sweating, and his jaws felt cramped.

He wondered if he'd been successful at keeping Tee Doyle out of his head.

He sure as hell hoped so. Hoped she didn't know she'd just described the nightmare he'd been having off and on since he was seven years old.

Chapter 4

That night he had the dream again, for the first time in…he didn't know how long. A couple of years. After Matt's accident, maybe?

It started the way it always did, him dreaming of waking up in the darkness, of being afraid, terrified. Heart racing and pounding, he was sweating and shaking, wanting to cry but knowing he was too big to cry. He didn't want to be a baby, did he? He didn't cry, he *didn't.* But his chest and throat hurt as if he did.

Then the noise. Terrible noises—things crashing, breaking; thumps and bangs, voices yelling…screaming. A man's voice yelling. A woman's voice screaming.

My mother's voice.

Yes. This time he knew it was his mother's voice—the screaming…crying…begging.

There were other voices, too, small frightened voices—
not mine!—whimpering, "Mommy..."

And finally...finally the *other* voice, the one he'd been
waiting for, praying for, soft as a breath blowing warm
past his ear. *Shh... It's okay...it's gonna be okay. I won't
let him hurt you. Nobody's gonna hurt you. You're safe
now. It's okay...*

He felt safe, then, and warm, and when the loudest
noises came, he crouched down in the warm darkness and
waited for the crashing and banging and screaming and
yelling to stop and the lights to turn on, so bright they hurt
his eyes. So bright he always woke up.

Once, when he was a kid, he'd told Matt about the
dream. When he got to the part about the soft voice, Matt
had nodded emphatically, the way those little bobblehead
dogs do that people put in their cars. "I remember that,"
he'd said. "It was the angel."

Wade, being older and past believing in angels, but
kindhearted enough not to want to hurt his little brother's
feelings, merely asked, "How do you know?"

"I just do," Matt replied. "He always came when I was
scared."

"He? A man angel? Aren't angels supposed to be ladies?"

"Uh-uh—not a man, a *boy* angel. Like us, only bigger.
Boys can be angels, because if a boy dies, what else is
he gonna be?"

That was a bit too much for Wade; it gave him a funny
feeling in his stomach. So he'd said, "Boys are too
ornery to be angels!" and pounced on Matt and tickled
him until he almost wet his pants and had to dash off to
the bathroom.

After that, when the bright lights came he'd tried to see the angel's face, but he always woke up before he could.

On this night, though, instead of going back to sleep, Wade lay thinking about the dream and Matt's "angel." Nothing had happened in his life so far to change his mind about the existence of angels, but… But *what?* He had dreams about a presence that comforted him in times of danger. His little brother had an imaginary "angel" who did the same thing for him. He'd always chalked it up to bad dreams and Matt's vivid imagination, but evidently the presence was a powerful enough part of his own psyche that Tierney had picked up on it, and what did *that* mean? He had no memories of the years before he'd been adopted, which had happened when he was seven and Matt was five. Except…

Tonight he'd dreamed he heard his mother's voice. Was that just a dream, or was it a memory?

If it was a memory, what about the rest of the dream? Was that a memory, too?

If the whole dream was a memory, what was it about, all the screaming and the noise? As a cop he knew the sounds of violence when he heard them. Could something really bad have happened in his childhood that he'd blocked all memory of, except for this one recurring nightmare?

If so, who in the he—uh, heck—*is Matt's angel?*

The logical conclusion would be Mom or Dad, he supposed. But again, his experience in law enforcement told him that if Mom was the one doing the screaming, it was most likely Dad doing the shouting. And banging.

Wide awake and sweaty, heart pounding, Wade threw back the wreckage of his covers and got out of bed. A glance at the clock on the nightstand told him he could have taken another hour, but he knew better than to try to sleep. Instead he walked to the window, yawning and scratching, and peered out at the familiar shapes of his neighbors' houses, just becoming visible in the thinning darkness.

In the above-garage apartment he rented from a nice retired couple named Hofmeyer, the bedroom window overlooked the street while the kitchen and sitting room opened onto a deck at the back which enjoyed the nicer and more private view of the neighbors' trees, shrubs and flower gardens. He was about to turn and make his way to the bathroom to begin the process of making himself ready for polite company, when a slight movement caught his eye. He froze, eyes narrowed, zeroing in on the source of the movement, which hadn't come again. Nevertheless, in the rapidly approaching daylight he found it—someone sitting in a car parked directly across the street.

No reason to think anything about that. Could have been someone waiting for his neighbor, running late for their car pool. Could have been—aw, hell, he knew it wasn't any of the things it could have been. Maybe it was what Tierney had said about someone watching him, and the fact that he was beginning to have some respect for that lady's "impressions." That, and the feeling in his gut. The cop sense that had kept him out of serious trouble a couple of times in his career told him whoever it was sitting out there in his dark car in the breaking dawn was there because of *him*.

He eased back from the window so as not to alert the watcher by any sudden movements of his own. In the darkness of his bedroom he found the pair of pants he'd worn the day before—on the floor right where he'd stepped out of them—and slipped them on. Barefoot, he quick-timed it down the stairs and out the door that opened onto the Hofmeyer's backyard. There, he closed the door silently behind him and paused a moment to listen. Heard the far-off hum of traffic, still fitful at this hour. Some muffled breathing—his own. Some rustlings in trees and shrubbery that could have been just about anything, but nothing he needed to worry about. Satisfied the watcher hadn't yet taken alarm, he slipped around the corner of the garage and started down the flagstone pathway at a tiptoe run.

All was well, going his way. Right up until the moment his bare foot made contact with something large, warm and soft. As the object emitted a loud grunt, Wade went down—swearing, a succinct sibilance kept under his breath that probably wouldn't have been loud enough to raise alarms from the watcher across the street. He might have salvaged the situation even then if, in the natural reflexive action of someone in the process of falling, he hadn't flung out his arm and attempted to grab the nearest solid object. This happened to be the gate, or more accurately, the gate latch, which gave with a loud clang, allowing the gate to swing back against the wall of the garage with a resounding thump.

As he lay full-length and prone upon the flagstones, he heard a car's engine start up, then accelerate and move off down the street.

With a groan, he rolled over onto his back, then immediately wished he hadn't, as a pair of large stubby paws planted themselves squarely in the middle of his chest, and a long snout terminated by a large wet nose snuffled noisily across his face. Before he could get an arm up to fend it off, a very long, very wet tongue smelling of well-aged liver followed.

"Ah, jeez, Bruno..." This Wade uttered in a constricted wheeze, as the front half of a grossly overweight basset hound settled onto his chest. "Get...off, you lump of lard—your breath would gag a maggot, you know that?" In response to the insult Bruno turned his head away with studied disdain, one ear slapping Wade across the face in the process. "What are you doing out here, you good-for-nothing fleabag? You let some stranger sit right there across the street and spy on me? Some watchdog *you* are."

As if to contradict that, Bruno lifted his nose to the dawn sky and uttered a halfhearted, "Ah-rooo..." Then he proceeded across Wade's body with all the grace of an elephant climbing over a picket fence.

"Someday..." Wade snarled as a well-padded tail slapped his face in a disdainful wave of farewell. However, the threat went unspoken as his senses picked up an indescribably foul odor wafting back from the animal now waddling unhurriedly off down the flagstone pathway.

"Ah, *jeez!*" was all Wade could manage while coughing and swearing blasphemously. He fought his way to his feet in hopes of finding some less polluted air, and since the gate was open anyway, he darted through it and down the driveway to the street.

But of course the watcher—if that's who it was—was long gone.

Wade went back to his apartment to shower and dress for work, mad enough to chew up nails and spit out bullets. Not even the shower on full cold did much to settle the steam.

Damn it, he didn't need this! He had a serial—now cop—killer on the loose and a city on full alert, a beautiful psychic giving him nightmares and now he'd picked up a stalker? What the hell was going on?

By the time he'd emerged from the shower and scrubbed himself pink, he'd resolved a couple of things. One: last time he'd looked, by God, the name plate on his desktop said *Detective* Callahan. So it was high time he got off his ass and started detecting. Which meant getting the answers to a whole lot of questions. And two: he had a feeling the person with the answers to some of those questions was the beautiful psychic, the same one responsible for his most recent nightmares.

Which made his first move of the morning a no-brainer: he needed to talk to the psychic.

He probably shouldn't have been surprised when he wiped the steam off of the mirror and saw a smile on his beard-stubbled face. Well, hell, he thought, whistling tunelessly as he picked up his shaver, it's a terrible job, but *somebody* has to do it....

"Hi, honey, it's me."

"Cory! Wow, it's really early out there. Where are you? What's—is anything wrong? Did you see him? Talk to him? How did it go? For heaven's sake, *say* something, damn it. I've been waiting all night for you to call."

"Samantha, dearest, I will say something if you'll let me."

"Okay." There was a pause, and some heavy breathing. "I'm shutting up now. Your turn."

"Well then, to answer your questions in order. I'm sitting in a rental car—a Honda Civic, I think—in the parking lot of a Holiday Inn. Nothing's wrong. Yes, I saw him. No, I didn't talk to him, and it didn't 'go' at all."

"Okay...and you are about to tell me why, right, Pearse?"

"I chickened out, Sam." His wife, understanding him well and knowing how fragile he was right now, didn't press. He laughed the way people do when nothing's funny, drew in a breath and blew it out audibly. "I feel like a complete idiot, but I couldn't do it. I drove up and parked across the street from the house. I could see a light on in his apartment, so I knew he was home. And I couldn't make myself go in there."

"Oh, Cory."

"The guy's a cop, Sam. Those guys are hard-wired to be suspicious. What's he going to do when some stranger walks up to him and says, 'Hi, I'm your big brother'? A brother he hasn't seen since he was six years old and probably doesn't remember. At this point I have no proof. Nothing whatsoever to back that up."

"What about Holt Kincaid? His files—"

"...Will document a search based on *my* knowledge that I have four siblings somewhere in this world. Wade Callahan evidently has no such knowledge. According to his employment and school records, he's only got one brother, a year and a half younger, named Matthew. I can't just spring this on him, not until I have something to offer besides my crazy story." He gave a brief snort of laughter. "If I keep up like I've been doing, he's liable to shoot me for a burglar or arrest me for stalking."

"What do you mean, like you've been doing? What did you do?"

"What did I do? I sat in front of his house in my car, that's what I did. And this morning he almost caught me."

"You sat in your *car?* All *night?* Good Lord, Pearse,

you're an investigative journalist. You've covered wars, revolutions, genocide, interviewed terrorists, dictators, heads of state. And you're telling me—"

"He's my little brother, Sam."

There was a long pause, then a sigh. "I know, love."

"I let him down."

"Cory, you didn't. He was taken away from you. You were a child yourself. What could you have done?"

"I should have found a way. I was supposed to protect them—all of them. And I let them split us up. Now…I've got a chance to get us back together."

"You will, Pearse. I know you will."

"But I have to do this right. I can't screw it up, Sam. This time I have to get it *right.*"

Wade arrived at the downtown station out of sorts and running late, nursing a sore elbow and limping slightly, thanks to the contact—harder than first realized—a couple of his appendages had made with the flagstones during his early morning foray. The task force was assembled in the briefing room, evidently waiting for him, which right away ticked him off.

Ed Francks handed him a black armband when he walked in, then gave him a sideways look that slid down to his gimpy leg and back up again. Being wise and experienced, the older man didn't say anything.

One of the younger detectives, though, an import from the northeast named Rudy…something Italian, apparently wasn't smart enough to follow the veteran cop's lead. He sang out, "Hey, Boss, what happened to your leg?" and for his concern got a glare that would have frozen up Old Faithful.

"In the first place, Detective, I'm not your boss," Wade growled, then expanded the glare to take in the rest of the room. "What is this, *kindergarten?* You gotta have your teacher hold your hand before you can go to the john?"

There was some uneasy stirring and shifting around, but nobody said anything.

Muttering to himself, Wade turned his back on the lot of them while he slipped the armband up his sleeve. This brought him face to face with the board, upon which the latest crime scene photos had already been posted. Above these, and partly obscuring the most grisly, someone had tacked a large photograph of Officer Alicia Williams in her dress uniform. She was smiling, her slightly slanted black eyes sparkling beneath the brim of her hat, looking like she had the world by the tail and a good life ahead of her.

Damn.

He took a deep breath, tapped the photograph, then turned. "All right, ladies and gentlemen, in case anybody needs reminding, this is why we're here. What may or may not be wrong with my leg is not the business of this task force. Finding a killer—now a *cop* killer—is. Now, somebody want to be the first to tell me I've got reason to believe we might catch this sonofabitch today?"

After that the briefing proceeded along pretty much normal lines. Reports: canvases had turned up no witnesses, autopsy results were roughly the same as with all the other victims; CSI had found no useful trace evidence on or near the victim. The remnants of Officer Williams's burned uniform were being processed for DNA, which would take a while—a lot longer than it did on TV forensics procedurals, for sure.

Family members and friends of the earlier victims were being re-interviewed to determine whether any of them ever had occasion to wear a uniform, on the job or off. Results so far: vic number three, the retired schoolteacher, had been working part-time as a crossing guard at a busy intersection near her house. Vic number two was a city bus driver, and yes, they wore uniforms. Vic number one, the former army private turned college student, had been supplementing her G.I. Bill working nights as a security guard at a popular downtown nightclub.

Wade nodded. "Number five—that's the docent. Six, Officer Williams. We have anything for number four?"

"Working on it," Rudy the Italian muttered, thumbing through his notes.

Wade stared at the notes he'd scrawled on the board, and an old familiar tingle crawled up his backbone. There was something here. He was close, he knew it. If he could only... He wondered if Tierney might... Ah, hell. What was he doing? Using the woman as a crutch instead of depending on his own intelligence? She'd given him the uniform connection, what more did he want?

The uniform connection. He's timid, a mouse, Tierney said. He's most likely been abused by someone wearing a uniform. It represents oppression to him. What if...

He rapped a knuckle on the board where he'd written each victim's occupation involving a uniform, then jerked around to face the room.

"How 'bout this," he said, his voice strong and certain for the first time in a while—since this case had been handed to him. "Each of these victims would have been in a position to confront someone, cause them trouble, interfere with their plans, give them grief. Right? Maybe the bus driver won't let somebody on her bus because he doesn't have exact change. The museum docent…hell, I don't know, maybe she makes someone put out a cigarette, or chews him out for taking flash photos. You guys doing the interviews—go back and ask if they know if any of the victims reported trouble with anyone recently."

"Wait…I got something here—" Rudy had been flipping frantically back through his notes. "Yeah…right here. First victim's mom mentioned something about an altercation at the club the weekend before she was killed. Some guy gave her a hard time because she wouldn't let him in."

Wade exhaled gustily. "Okay. Say, the club doorkeeper denies our killer entrance. Ticks him off. She was the first vic—that could have been the trigger." He snapped his fingers, his mind racing now, almost too fast for his mouth to keep pace. "Okay, Rudy, stay on those interviews. Ochoa and Washburn, go back through Officer Williams's traffic citations over the last few weeks. Eliminate everybody that doesn't fit the profile—that would be women, men with families—wives and kids. Anybody over fifty."

Martin Ochoa, who'd been busily scribbling notes, lifted his head. "So, we got a profile now? When did we come up with that?"

Ochoa's partner from Robbery-Homicide, Larry Washburn, nudged him and grinned. "I bet he got it from his crystal ball. Hey, Callahan, where is that crystal ball of yours today?"

Wade gave that the response it deserved, which was a stone-cold stare. "May I remind all of you comedians that Ms. Doyle is a civilian who has graciously volunteered her talents and time to help apprehend a killer? A killer who's killed six times. Anyone who wants to sit around here making cracks better hope there isn't a seventh."

At that point Nola Hoffman stuck her head in to remind Wade about the news conference about to commence, and at which his presence was requested. Meaning required.

"Be right down, Boss." Wade swore under his breath while Nola's high heels went tap-tapping off down the hallway, then turned back to his team. "Okay, you've got your work cut out for you. Let's focus on getting this guy before he kills again. We're looking for a young male, late twenties, early thirties, single, a loner, probably works some kind of menial job. Most likely a rep for not playing well with others. That's all—unless you plan on sitting around here on your asses all day."

Glowering, he headed off to join the mayor's news conference. Trying his best not to limp.

Wade's role in this as in all the other news conferences he'd been called upon to attend, was to stand at parade rest beside Nola, two steps behind and a little to one side of Chief Cutter and Alan Styles, and attempt to strike an attitude somewhere between alert and somber. The mayor would make his speech, then introduce Chief Cutter, who would bark out a quotable phrase or two, then waste no time in turning the microphone over to the chief of special cases. Styles would do most of the talking, including fielding questions from the news media.

Thus his mind was not exactly tuned in to the proceedings until he caught the end of a question from one of the network TV reporters that brought him back to front and center in a hurry.

"—true the department has been working with a psychic on this case?"

Chief Styles, naturally, declined to comment on "the details of an ongoing investigation," and pointed to a waving hand on the other side of the crowd.

The reporter, who hadn't earned her network stripes by being so easily brushed off, shouted over the babble, "Chief, we have reports from a reliable source that the psychic credited with helping solve the Yreka kidnapping last year has been seen both here and at the last two crime scenes. Care to comment on *that?*"

Styles, who'd never gotten the hang of out-and-out lying to the press, covered the mic with one hand while he bent his head to confer with Chief Cutter. Then he turned and looked at Nola, who jabbed Wade in the ribs with her elbow and growled, "Take it, Callahan."

He uttered one short, sharp cussword under his breath, then stepped up to the mic. Cleared his throat. "We always welcome any useful information from members of the community. Members of the media included."

That got a bit of a chuckle, and Wade was about to step back when a voice he knew, belonging to the regular police reporter for the *Portland Oregonian,* sang out, "Come on, Callahan, rumor says you've got your own personal crystal ball."

Ducking his head to the mic once more, Wade scowled at the crowd and snapped, "Wish I did. I'd sure as hell use it. We'll take help from anybody and anything if it'll help us catch this guy."

On that note, Chief Cutter stepped in and ended the news conference, although the clamor continued for several more minutes. Under its cover, Nola said dryly, "You shoulda been in politics, Callahan."

He was trying to think of a response to that when he felt his cell phone vibrating in its holster against his hip. He pulled it out, scowled at a number he didn't recognize, thumbed it on and barked, "Callahan." And heard a voice he did recognize, hushed and breathless.

"Wade, he's *there*. Right now. Somewhere close. I—"

"Hold on—*who's* here? You mean, *here* here—at this news conference? The *killer?*"

"No! At least…I haven't picked anything up. But I'm getting that Watcher again. Only he's…different. I don't know how to explain it, he's just as intense as before, but it feels different, somehow. Like it's a different person. And…before there was this exultation, this elation. Now I'm getting sadness. Really terrible sadness—like grief…"

Wade was only half listening, eyes sweeping the slowly dispersing crowd. The sun was in his eyes, having just broken through the morning overcast with all the intensity of a Portland summer day. It was only May, but it was going to be a warm one—humid, too. But *damn*. Nobody stood out. Nobody caught his attention. Nobody stared at him, or even lingered behind the rest of the horde.

"Miss Tee," he said, interrupting her, "we need to talk. What are you doing for lunch?"

Chapter 5

"Well," Tierney said, "I, uh, nothing. I guess."

Why had she lied?

She'd planned to go to the Rose Gardens. Damn it, she *needed* to go to the Rose Gardens. There'd been too much sadness in her mind these past few days. Too much ugliness. She craved the nurturing beauty of the flowers and the blissful waves of happy feelings she could always count on finding among the beds of blooming roses.

"Good," Wade said, "I'll pick you up. Fifteen minutes."

An unaccustomed bolt of temper shot through her. "Wait! Wade—"

It was too late; the phone clicked in her ear and he was gone. Angrily, she thumbed Redial.

"Yeah, what?" He sounded vexed, impatient.

"Actually," she said sweetly, "I'd planned to go to the

Rose Gardens. I've made myself a sandwich to take along. If you want to talk to me, bring something for yourself and meet me there. Twenty minutes." She clicked the phone off.

Almost immediately it rang in her hand. She thumbed it on and said, "Yeah, what?" in a deliberate parody of his abrupt manner.

The chuckle in her ear was repentant. "Okay, sorry. Where shall I meet you? Washington Park's a big place."

"The gift shop's fine. It's—"

"I know where it is. Okay, see you there in twenty minutes."

This time, holding the silent phone in her hand, she felt triumphant but giddy. No mystery why; she was meeting a man for lunch, which was enough of a rarity all by itself. Add to that the fact that he was attractive, sort of…in an odd, tough-guy kind of way…

No. None of that was relevant. Except for the fact that *she* was attracted to *him.*

Yes, that was what made it an occasion for giddiness and wonder. She was allowing herself to have lunch with a man to whom she very definitely felt attracted.

For most of her adult life she'd made it a practice to avoid close relationships of all kinds, even friendships with other women. With people who knew about her "gift," there was the inevitable awkwardness, and with those who didn't, the strain of trying to maintain her secret. It had seemed simpler to keep her distance, to keep relationships casual, except for Jeannette, of course, the only family she had.

And now Jeannette was slipping away from her. Soon she would be truly alone.

It came as something of a shock to her to realize she was

lonely. Had she always been? Was she able to see it only now because there was this person in her life so vital, so dynamic, so complex that he took up a huge amount of space when he was with her, and left an equally huge emptiness when he wasn't? Or was it true—as she'd read somewhere—that loneliness had less to do with the number of people in your life than it did the absence of a particular one?

If either of those possibilities was true, Tierney realized, she was in big trouble. Because Detective Wade Callahan, no matter how stimulating his company or how attracted to him she felt, was in her life on a professional basis only, and a temporary one, at that. She'd take care, as she always had, that neither he nor anyone else would ever become anything more. So, she supposed she'd better get used to being lonely.

But for now, she was meeting a man for lunch at the Rose Gardens, and for that, she decided, she would allow herself the sweet effervescence of anticipation. She would put on lipstick and a bright spring sundress in a shade of blue that brought out the color of her eyes. She would wear sandals with a bit of a heel that made her legs look long and shapely. She would smile. What harm could it do, for these few moments, to forget The Gift and simply be happy in a man's company?

If only such a thing were possible.

She made it to the Rose Gardens's gift shop in less than twenty minutes, but he'd managed to get there ahead of her. In the manner of men everywhere, as he waited he paced, fidgeting, a paper bag from a fast-food place in one hand, the other in his pocket except when he pulled it out every few seconds to glance at his wrist.

She didn't mean to listen in on his unguarded emotions, but his pacing path had taken him away from the entrance to the gardens, so he was unaware of her approach and therefore unshielded. And too far away to call to without making a spectacle of them both. She would have expected impatience, even annoyance, given his earlier mood—in her experience, all men seemed to hate waiting. But if he did feel any of that it was being overshadowed by darker, fiercer emotions. Waves of frustration too strong to have been caused by a few minutes' wait. Flashes of violence. Islands of tragedy in a sea of emptiness. A complex puzzle with too many pieces missing for her to see what it was about.

Her steps faltered, then quickened as she hurried to get close enough to him to call out. Her jaws tightened as she struggled to smile. She was determined to smile.

"Wade—hello!"

He executed an almost comical about-face, and she felt instant relief from the emotional barrage. As he strolled lazily toward her the smile on his face revealed nothing but the pleasure of a man greeting a woman on a beautiful spring day. His feelings were completely shielded from her now, so she couldn't even be sure if the pleasure and the smile were real.

To avoid the almost certain awkwardness of their meeting like this, she gestured toward the fast-food bag he was holding and said, "Was that the best you could do?"

He arched his eyebrows. "Hey, I'm a manly man. I require red meat." He shrugged and added, "Besides, it was on the way."

He motioned toward the camera hanging around her neck. "I see you came armed."

"It's the reason I wanted to come here, actually. I needed more rose photos. I use them for my paintings, and with the Rose Festival coming up I have to have plenty ready to sell."

She didn't mention the part about needing the healing powers of the place, and was surprised when he said softly, "Is that the only reason?"

Something quickened inside her, and she squinted and put up a hand to shield her eyes, though not from the sun. "What do you mean?"

"Oh, I don't know…just that you said this was a place where most of the feelings floating around are happy ones. I figured, after the past couple of days, you might be needing some of that about now."

She couldn't answer him—didn't know what to say. She felt idiotic to be so touched by his words. And by the fact that it seemed he'd gone beyond just believing in her gift and was even beginning to understand it.

The awkward moment stretched, and as such moments often do, ended when both of them spoke at the same time. Tierney said, "What did you want—" and Wade said, "I guess we should—" and it was Tierney who yielded with a small self-conscious laugh.

"Eat first," Wade said firmly. "Then talk."

He'd almost forgotten what he'd come for. The watcher in the car outside his apartment this morning, who may or may not have been present at the news conference at police headquarters—it had all faded into background noise the moment he'd turned and seen her coming toward him, the sun making a halo of her hair and painting roses on her cheeks, her rapid pace stirring breezes that flirted with her skirt and teased him with the suggestion of long, slender thighs beneath…

Hey, dumb ass, she's not your type, remember? A voice somewhere in the back of his mind tried to get his attention. *Too complicated! She reads minds!*

Uh-uh—not minds, emotions. And his were under tight rein. He'd made sure of that.

They decided to eat lunch in a picnic area in the park near the gardens. Tierney chose a reasonably clean table and Wade dusted it off with some of the abundance of napkins he'd grabbed to go with his burger. He tried to remember the last time he'd eaten a meal outdoors under trees with a beautiful woman, and couldn't. He made a mental note to do it more often, assuming he could find a woman willing to go along.

He hauled the fries out of the bag first, as always, and managed to get a couple of ketchup packets opened before he lost patience and went after the main course. He was about to bite into his burger with his usual gusto when his attention was claimed by the woman across the table from him.

He watched, his own lunch poised halfway to his mouth, as she unwrapped the foil from an untidy mound of just about every vegetable he'd ever heard of—tomatoes, avocados, cucumbers, some kind of sprouts, and God only knew what else—barely contained between two slices of seriously healthy and crunchy-looking brown bread. His eyes followed, his breathing held in suspense, as she carefully lifted this monster to her mouth, closed her eyes and took a hefty bite. There was a distinct crunch, followed by a soft moan of pleasure.

Wade's stomach gave a loud growl. He just managed to get his mouth closed before her eyes opened wide and focused on him.

"Hmm?" she asked, smiling with closed lips in a way that reminded him of a contented cat.

"Nothing." Which was the only thing he could say without opening up doors between them that were better left shut.

She chewed, swallowed, picked an errant wisp of sprouts from her lips, then said with a shrug, "You were probably going to say something snarky about my sandwich—and that's not by benefit of my 'gift', by the way. Merely what most men would say, I suspect."

"Maybe I'm not 'most men,'" he said with a certain arrogance, and with veiled eyes and a shrug of his own. Then he looked up at her and smiled. "Not that it surprises me. I should've guessed you'd be a vegetarian."

"I'm not a vegetarian. Not totally," she managed to say through another bite. "I just forgot to go grocery shopping. With everything that's been…" She let that trail off into silence, and he knew she regretted being the one to invite the shadows back.

They ate in silence, then, and she waited until she'd finished her sandwich and he'd polished off his burger and tapped into his diet soda before she reminded him why they were there. She twisted the top off a bottle of water, took a sip, then quietly asked, "So? What did you want to talk to me about?"

He squeezed a glob of ketchup onto the wrapper from his burger, picked up a small bouquet of French fries and dabbed them into the ketchup, thinking it didn't seem right, somehow, to be talking of nightmares and sinister watchers and serial killers in such a setting. Wishing he could enjoy the respite *she* found in this place.

But the world, particularly the part of it he lived in, wasn't a rose garden.

He frowned at the ketchup-draped fries, popped them all into his mouth and went on frowning while he chewed and thought about how to ask the questions swirling like dry leaves in his mind.

Who the hell is stalking me, and why? Is it somebody from one of my cases? From this *case?*

Why am I having The Dream again?

"I suppose," said Tierney, casually helping herself to one of his fries, "you want to know more about The Watcher. I'm not 'reading' you," she added, fixing her candid blue eyes on his face. "It pretty much has to be that or the case, and if it was the case, you'd probably have asked me to meet you at police headquarters. And—" she popped the French fry into her mouth and munched for a moment "—you wouldn't find it so hard to talk about."

He confirmed that with a mirthless laugh. "Nice deduction, Sherlock. Okay, yeah, I want to know about this… watcher, stalker, or whoever he is. It *is* a he, right?"

"I think so." She tilted her head, considering. "Yes—I'm pretty sure it's a man. Or…men."

"And you're not picking up on what the guy—or guys—want?"

"No…but—"

"But *what?* If you know anything about this, *tell me, damn it.*"

"I don't get any sense of anger, or hate—anything that suggests he means you harm. Quite the opposite, in fact.

He seems… I don't know, I just keep picking up this sense of *longing*. Of terrible sadness mixed in with great happiness. Happiness that he's found you, I guess. About the sadness…I'm not sure." She paused, and he watched a tinge of pink wash into her cheeks.

"What?" he demanded again. "Whatever it is, tell me."

She shook her head, smiling faintly. "I don't know how you're going to take this, but what he seems to feel for you is…love."

"Ah, jeez." He gave a snort of disgust and began gathering up the remnants of lunch and stuffing them into the fast-food bag. "Now you're creeping me out, Miss Tee. Seriously. This is *all* I need."

Her smile widened, to his further annoyance, but at least she had the good sense not to comment. Instead she added her trash to his and looped her camera around her neck, then gathered her skirt into one hand, giving him a brief glimpse of slender legs while she lifted them to swivel around on the picnic bench.

"I really need to get some pictures before it heats up and the blossoms start to droop," she said, standing and brushing at the back of her skirt. "Do you want to walk with me?"

He hesitated, knowing very well he should get back to the job. But he didn't want to leave. Not yet. And not because he hadn't really gotten the answers to his questions. *Not about the nightmare. No, not that one.*

He didn't know how to tell her about the watcher outside his apartment that morning. And about the nightmare. Or maybe he just didn't want to tell her, for the same reason he didn't want to go back to work. Because it was nice being here with her like this, not thinking about the ugliness of the job, or the violence and turmoil of the night-mare. Not thinking about the unanswered questions that kept his muscles tied up with tension and his nerves on edge. Right here, right now, he felt a strange lassitude, something so unfamiliar to him he wasn't even certain he could call it by its right name.

Peace? Contentment?

It was dangerous, *that* he knew. Peace and contentment weren't things a homicide detective on a case needed to be wallowing in.

He got up from the table and carried the remains of their lunch to the nearest trash barrel, dusted off his hands and turned to Tierney, the necessary words of parting forming in his mind. She was waiting for him a few yards away, her head turned toward him, seconding her invitation with a smile along one bare, lightly freckled shoulder. He felt an odd little hitch in his breathing, and the words in his mind melted away, dried up, like the first raindrops on hot pavement.

What the hell, he thought. *A few more minutes isn't going to matter much, one way or the other.*

They walked back to the gardens side-by-side, not hurrying, not talking, just strolling the way people do when they don't want the walk to end, but can't say the things they need to say.

Until Tierney took an audible breath and said, "Can I ask *you* a question?"

He glanced at her, feeling mellow enough to say, "Sure, go ahead."

"What happened to make you feel you needed to talk to me?" She paused, but not long enough for him to reply.

"Something did happen, didn't it? Something that upset you *before* I called and told you about The Watcher being at the news conference."

His denial was automatic. "I wasn't upset, I just—" He broke it off with some whispered swearing, shaking his head, looking at the ground. "I can't get away with anything with you, can I?"

"Oh, I think you can," she said, and he heard a smile in her voice. "When you want to. But you want to tell me this. You just don't quite know how."

"Okay," he admitted after some more muttered blasphemy, "you're right, I did want to tell you." He held up a hand. "But I wasn't *upset*. Just ticked off. Weirded-out. Or something. Not upset. I don't *get* upset." He took a deep breath. And purposely didn't look at her, knowing for sure she'd be smiling.

"All right, it was just a dream I had. One I've had before, going way back to when I was a kid. Hadn't had it in a long time, though, and then yesterday you told me you'd picked up…something from me. Something about…violence. Terror, you said. Something bad happening that scared me pretty bad, but you said there was somebody there…" He had to stop, wasn't sure why, suddenly he just couldn't go on.

"The Protector," Tierney said softly. "Someone who made you feel safe."

"Yeah." He said it on an exhalation, then ran a hand over his hair. "The thing is, that pretty much is my dream. The one I've been having since I was a kid. Last night I had it again, only this time I heard my mother's voice. I told you I don't have any memories from before I was adopted, and that was the truth. But I do have this dream, and now I'm starting to think it might be some kind of memory." He paused, and this time she didn't attempt to fill the silence, just waited for him to continue. "Anyway, like I said, I heard my mother's voice. Only she's not the protector. She's…the *violence*. The terror—part of it, anyhow." His jaws tightened, and he could hear the hard edge in his voice. "I'm pretty sure I know what it was, that part of it. Domestic violence is something I've learned a lot about, in my line of work. Unfortunately. What I still don't get, though, is the part about this…protector."

"You never see who it is? In the dream, I mean."

He shook his head. "It's dark. Then someone comes and turns the lights on, so bright they blind me—hurt my eyes. And I always wake up before I can see the person—the protector's face." He gave a short laugh. "I assume it's a person. My little brother insisted it was an angel."

Tierney smiled, lifted her camera and zoomed in on a cluster of yellow blossoms tinged with blush pink. A man on the opposite side of the rose bed checked, then moved quickly a few steps farther on so as not to ruin her shot. Then he paused to lift his camera, too.

She checked the viewing screen, then glanced up at Wade. "So then…you woke up?"

"Yeah. It was early, just barely starting to get light. But I figured there wasn't any point in going back to sleep, so I got up. I went over to the windows and looked out at the street—I don't know, I always do that first thing when I get up. Force of habit. Anyway, I spotted a car parked across the street, and a guy was sitting in it."

Tierney lowered her camera and frowned. They'd moved on to another rose bed, this one a cream and red bicolor, a favorite of hers. On the edge of her field of vision, she saw the man with the camera stoop to smell one of the fragrant blossoms. Waves of contentment and pleasure wafted across the bed like perfume. She relaxed and murmured, "The Watcher?"

"It was the first thing I thought of. Call me paranoid if you want to, but in my line of work paranoia's a good thing. A little paranoia can keep you alive. Anyway, I tried to catch the guy—ask him what the hell he was doing parked in front of my house in the dark of the morning—but he drove off before I—" He broke off and ran a hand over his close-cropped hair. "Hell, I blew it, that's all."

She felt his chagrin and embarrassment and knew better than to ask why or how. "And then a few hours later," she mused, "The Watcher shows up at your news conference."

Her mind was only half on what she was saying; she'd deliberately chosen a path that would intersect with the stranger's, and the distance between them was closing rapidly. Would he step aside and try to avoid her? Or—no, he was standing in the pathway gazing at the sea of glorious blossoms, his face alight with...

Joy. Love. Nostalgia.

The man was immersed in memories, happy ones.

He came to himself as Tierney and Wade approached, and looked around, appearing startled. But with a friendly smile, saying, as he stepped quickly aside, "Oh—sorry, am I in your way?"

He had a nice voice, mellow and rich. A nice face, too. And kind eyes. But, Tierney thought, there was something weary about them, too, as if they'd seen much that was neither nice nor kind.

She and Wade both made polite assurances, but the stranger's smile grew wry with apology.

"I have to plead guilty to not paying attention. All this— these roses takes me back a bit. The first time I saw my wife was in a rose garden."

He's holding something back, Tierney thought. *A private memory, something delicious...*

"Really? Where was that?"

To her surprise it was Wade who picked up the conversational ball, at the same time throwing her a glance that had *question* pouring out of it like water from a faucet. She didn't read minds, but she knew he was asking her for her "take" on the stranger.

It frustrated her to admit she didn't have one—not one she trusted. He seemed benign, but at the same time...

How odd. It's almost as if...he has the same bits and pieces missing as Wade. The same fragments of violence and danger that pop into his gentler emotions now and then, like gunfire way off in the distance.

"Washington," the stranger said, and quickly added, "D.C., not state."

"Ah," said Wade. "That where you're from?"

"No, but my job takes me there a lot. Among other places. I'm a journalist, by the way—Cory Pearson." He held out his hand.

"Wade Callahan—I'm a cop," Wade said as he took it.

"Really? Here? In Portland?"

He knows that, Tierney thought, *but it doesn't alarm him.* Then two "impressions" hit her simultaneously.

Love!

Lies!

She knew the man was hiding his true self, holding himself in check, guarding emotions so powerful he couldn't quite contain them.

She opened her mouth to say something, anything to get Wade's attention, but the words wouldn't come. The force of the "impressions" had literally taken her breath away.

The moment of paralysis passed, as it always did, and she was able to draw breath, and with it a little gasp that was the prelude to speech, to the warning she needed to give. But before she could speak she felt a timid touch on her arm. She turned to find an Asian man standing there, shyly holding out his camera and pointing to himself and then to his large family, nodding and smiling at her from a short distance away.

As Tierney took the man's camera and followed him to where his family had assembled for a photo in front of a bed of roses in full and glorious bloom, she heard the stranger—Cory Pearson—say to Wade, "Hey, there's a thought—would you mind? For my wife. She'll love this…"

Her mind was in turmoil, trying to concentrate on two things at once and failing to keep up with either one. The Asian family was patient with her hesitation, thinking she was having trouble understanding their camera. They were all chattering helpfully at her and pointing to this button and that one. Meanwhile, she could hear Wade and the stranger talking together in low-key but friendly tones as Wade obligingly took several photos with the man standing in front of different varieties of roses, then one with the city and Mount Hood in the distant background.

And all the time they were moving farther and farther away from her.

By the time the family had run out of poses, reclaimed their camera and moved on, she was ready to weep with frustration. She turned to look for Wade, keeping one hand clasped to her forehead, which had begun to ache from the pressure of her silently screamed—and futile—warnings.

She spotted him at last on the lower level, idly strolling and obviously alone. And watching for her, because as soon as he saw her looking his way he lifted a hand and started toward her. She hurried to meet him, then broke into a run—probably not the wisest move, given the sandals she was wearing. She watched his attitude change from relaxed to alert as he read the urgency on her face, saw him quicken his step and reach for her in time to keep her from plunging headlong into his arms.

"Whoa," he said as he steadied her, holding her firmly by the arms.

Heat and strength enveloped her, and a rich masculine aura filled her senses, and she felt safe…*protected.* It was what *he'd* felt, she realized, as a child and in his dreams. It felt so wonderful, for a moment she wanted to weep like a child herself, a child finding shelter in loving arms.

"What's the matter? Something happen, or did you just pick up on somebody's crisis?"

She struggled to shake off the emotions, gulp back the threatening tears, and managed to achieve a semblance of calm. "Where is he? The man with the camera—where did he go?"

"I don't know—moved on, I guess. Why? Did you—"

"Yes. We have to find him. Wade—I'm almost sure he's The Watcher."

Chapter 6

"You're sure about this? No mistake?"

Tierney gave Wade a quick glance and said jerkily, "I know what I felt." She was out of breath from walking rapidly, trying to keep up with him as they'd scoured every inch of the rose garden.

She'd long ago taken off her shoes and was carrying them in one hand, dangling by the heel straps. As she lifted the shoes in order to wipe the back of her hand against a trickle of sweat creeping down her forehead, Wade eyed the shoes and frowned.

"Look, there's no point in running all over the place. He's gone by now anyway."

She halted and let her shoulders slump. "Wade, I'm sorry. I should have—"

"Not your fault." It was the same thing he'd said the first

eight or so times she'd apologized. And she still didn't believe it.

"I picked it up when he shook your hand. I could have said something then, but there was that family wanting me to take their pictures. I should have just told them no, or I didn't understand, or *something*."

"Forget it. We've got his name, anyway—assuming he gave us the right one. Cory Pearson—jeez, a *journalist?* And you're *sure* he's the one. You didn't just pick up somebody else's emotions that happened to be floating around? You did say they have weddings here. The whole place is probably lousy with love."

She lifted her hand—and the shoes—again, this time in an unsuccessful attempt to catch the bubble of laughter that burst from her lips.

Wade threw her a look and said, "What's funny?"

She shook her head, still smiling, knowing it would be pointless to say, "Nothing." Knowing she couldn't possibly tell him how ridiculously happy it made her feel that he believed in her gift.

Although…it was a happiness so fragile that even recognizing its existence was enough to destroy it. What was she thinking? To let anyone's opinion of her matter so much was unwise. To allow any man's belief or disbelief to have the power to affect her happiness was just stupidity. To let *this* man's acceptance mean so much was both of those things to the nth degree. It was lunacy. Dangerous. Sheer insanity.

"It's just funny to hear you say that," she said as her smile grew wry, "as if you actually believe me. A couple days ago you felt quite a bit differently about me, I think." It was a compromise, of sorts.

He seemed to accept it, gave his own short bark of laughter, then frowned as he thought about it. "I'm still not sure about the psychic stuff, frankly," he said in a gruff, half-embarrassed tone. "You've got something, though— good instincts, people smarts—I don't know what it is, but I'd be a fool not to use it."

Which was a load of bull…whatever. He did believe. He believed in *her.* It was that simple.

Or that complicated.

"And speaking of that…have you got a few minutes?" He barely waited for her nod and murmured assent before putting his hand on her elbow and steering her toward the rose garden's exit. He glanced at the shoes in her hand and his frown deepened as he experienced an insane desire to pick her up and carry her. "Would you mind stopping by my place…see if you can pick up anything from the guy that was watching my apartment this morning? I don't live too far from here. Just take a minute."

"Okay, sure. Shall I follow you in my car or…"

"No sense in taking separate vehicles. I can drop you off here on my way back to the shop."

It *was* the most logistically sensible solution, he told himself, and had nothing to do with any reluctance he may or may not have felt about parting company with her.

He was careful to keep his vague sense of guilt blocked, but it accounted for the edge in his voice when he spoke to her, and the silence in the car on the way to his place.

It's police business, he told himself. He needed her in the car with him so he could get her impressions on the spot. But as he pulled up to the curb across the street from the Hofmeyers' 1930's style bungalow and parked in the approximate spot where the watcher's car had been this morning, he looked up at the windows of his apartment and his mind insisted on putting Tierney Doyle in the room behind those windows. In his bedroom. More precisely, in his bed. Naked. With her hair tousled on his pillow and her cheeks flushed and rosy and a very satisfied smile on her kiss-swollen lips. And her body...

He swore silently and earnestly. Shifted in his seat and twitched his suit jacket around to hide his growing discomfort as he looked over at Tierney. "Well? You getting anything?"

Damned if her cheeks weren't flushed and rosy, exactly like his daydream version, except she wasn't smiling. Her hands were knotted together in her lap and the shine in her eyes looked more like embarrassment than sexual fulfillment. *Lord help me,* he thought. *I tried to block it, I really did.*

"Um...I'm picking up some really strong emotions," Tierney said, "but I don't think they're from The Watcher." She cleared her throat and flashed him a small, tenuous smile. "I think somebody must be—" She put a hand over her eyes and muttered, "Lord, this is embarrassing...um, making love—really close by. Because all I can pick up is—"

"Yeah, yeah," Wade growled, "I get the picture." He did, too—all too well. Evidently some emotions *were* just too powerful to block.

"Wade, I'm sorry. I'm not getting anything else. That one—it's just that it's one of the most powerful emotions—"

"Yeah, right up there with killing," he said dryly as he reached for the ignition key.

He felt her eyes on him. "It's true. I hadn't thought

about it, but yes…two of the most powerful human emotions involve the creating of life, and the taking of it. But I do wish—"

"Forget it." *Please!* "It's not your fault."

Which was putting it mildly. He was pretty sure the idea of cavorting naked in his bedsheets would be the furthest thing from her mind.

And if he wasn't careful, thoughts like that could get him in a load of trouble. Charges of sexual harassment, at least. He'd have to watch himself from now on. He'd let himself get too damn comfortable with her today.

Picnicking with her, for God's sake. Couldn't let that happen again.

He drove her back to the Rose Garden to pick up her car with his elbow on the windowsill and his hand covering his mouth, angry with himself. And even though he remembered to block it, he knew from her troubled silence that Tierney still felt the anger and believed it was directed at her.

What the hell—it's better this way.

So why did he feel sick, sorry and sad, as if he'd just been involved in a lover's quarrel?

Wade had just draped his jacket over the back of his chair and was in the process of taking his cell phone and weapon out of their holsters when Ochoa and Washburn, the Robbery-Homicide twins, surrounded him. Ochoa dropped a short stack of papers on his desk, then hitched one hip onto a corner while Washburn took the visitor's chair beside it.

"What the hell's this?" Wade was in no mood for cryptic.

"Officer Williams's traffic citations that fit the 'profile.' And that's just for the last month," Washburn said.

Ochoa chimed in, "Evidently, the majority of traffic miscreants tend to fall into the category of young single males. Go figure."

Wade cut the stack of citations like a deck of cards and handed one to each of the detectives. "Okay, start running 'em down. See who's in the system for something worse than a traffic ticket. Check out the addresses. Check everything. See if anything jumps out. We're looking at somebody who's probably been in trouble as a juvenile. Maybe foster care."

Ochoa and Washburn looked at each other. Washburn, the comedian, said, "Job would go a lot faster if we split the pile three ways, boss."

Wade, who was already turning to his computer, swiveled back to glower at the pair, then gave an impatient "gimme" wave. "Okay, divvy up. I got something else to take care of first, though. Might take me a while…"

Wade waited until the two detectives had each slapped down a wad of citations and had gone off looking pleased with themselves, then brought up the Google screen, typed in "Cory Pearson journalist" and hit Search.

"Oh, Cory—you actually met him?" His wife's voice on the phone sounded choked-up, which naturally made his throat do the same.

"Yep," he said, grinning like an idiot. "I introduced myself and everything. Didn't mention the part about us being brothers, though."

There was a pause, and then, "You told him your name? Was that wise?"

"Well, I guess we'll see. I wanted—I don't know, I guess I was hoping it might jog a memory loose."

"Yes, but like you said, he's a cop. They're suspicious by nature. What if he decides to check you out?"

"Good—let him. Maybe *that* will bring something back. Although I'm not sure he's going to have a lot of time to devote to looking into my background, with this serial murder investigation they've got going here."

"I heard about that," Sam said. "It's made the national news."

"Yes," Cory said sadly. "Serial killings always do."

"Speaking of killing…" Sam's voice sounded sorrowful. "Your office called. Seems Beirut's exploded again. They want you there—yesterday."

He swore inventively, raked fingers through his hair and closed his eyes.

"He's not going anywhere, Pearse," his wife said gently. You know who he is and where he is. He'll still be there when you get back."

"Yeah, okay, you're right," he said on a long exhalation.

But he was a journalist who'd seen more of sudden death and young lives cut short than most people would in several lifetimes. Enough to know that what his wife had said wasn't always true.

The rest of the week passed the way Tierney's days always did. She tended the gallery, painted when she could, spent time picking up after Jeannette. And something new: tried not to think of Wade.

She thought about Wade a lot. There had been no more torture killings, and so no word from him, for which she was grateful on several counts—besides the obvious. She needed all the time she could squeeze out of every day to paint, getting ready for the Rose Festival. Or so she told herself. And she didn't like to leave Jeannette alone so much—she told herself that, too. Both of those things were true, but her biggest and best reason for being glad Wade hadn't called her—other than natural relief that no more women had suffered hideous deaths at the hands of a monster—was because she so badly wanted him to.

Although, *why* she should want to see him ever again was a mystery to her, after the way their picnic lunch at the Rose Gardens had ended.

She'd known immediately the erotic impressions she'd picked up were his—of course she had. And that she was the object of them—she'd known that, too. The feelings had been strong, clear and explicit, and as feelings like that did sometimes, they'd actually formed images in her mind. It wasn't the first time she'd picked up sexual fantasies involving her from men, and even, on a couple of occasions, from women. What was different about this time, and so unsettling to her, was the way she'd responded to them.

To him.

Usually when she picked up something blatantly sexual, she would throw up a mental block, remind herself it was normal and human to have such feelings, and ignore them. But *this* time… How had she let it happen? Had her guard been down? Or was it because she was attracted to him already? She tried not to ask herself those questions because every time she did it all came back—the way her heart had picked up his slow, heavy, sultry beat. The way the heat had spread through her body like lava, sizzling beneath her skin and settling in the lowest parts of her so that she felt both weighted and restless at the same time. The way she'd longed...ached...*needed* to be touched.

It had been a long time since she'd been touched that way.

Once in a while, she'd let *Why not?* cross her mind like a mouse making a daring dash over open floor.

But...no. The time wasn't right, and neither was he. A cop? Bad enough, as terrible at relationships as they were known to be. And this one with those missing pieces, missing memories, and skeletons in his closet even *he* didn't know about? *No.*

And besides that, there was Jeannette, who needed her more and more every day. These days Tierney had to help her grandmother with nearly everything, from getting dressed in the morning to going to bed at night. And in between there was the constant vigilance necessary to keep Jeannette from wandering off, hurting herself or setting the apartment on fire. Tierney had learned, sometimes the hard way, to keep anything that might cut, stab, poison, ignite, kindle, break, fall or tip over hidden or put away out of her grandmother's reach. Electrical outlets were covered by furniture that couldn't be easily moved, or taped over with duct tape. The knobs for the stove burners were hidden in a high cupboard, and all cupboard doors and drawers containing objects that might be dangerous or broken were locked with childproof fasteners. Windows and doors were kept locked, and the water heater was turned down to low.

But far, far worse than all that was losing the essential person that was *Jeannette.* Every day the shining light that had been her personality grew dimmer. Every day Tierney could feel the special link that had always been there between them becoming thinner, like a rubberband stretching…stretching. One day, she knew—probably soon—that bond would snap, and nothing would ever be able to put it back together. Her grandmother would be gone. Forever.

Sometimes, Tierney just had to go *somewhere*—the bathroom, or her workroom, or maybe the car—so she could cry.

No, this wasn't the time to be thinking about love, or even sex. And certainly not Wade.

As the days continued to roll by with no new victims, Wade and the other members of the TK—Torture Killer— Task Force grew more and more edgy. On the one hand, of course, everyone was relieved not to have to deal with another woman's brutalized body. But no new victims meant no new leads, no chance for new evidence or even, please Lord, a witness. And worse than that was the growing fear that the killer might have slipped through their fingers.

Since the news conference, the media had been all over what they'd delighted in calling the department's "crystal ball." So far Wade had managed to keep Tierney's home address secret, but there'd been plenty of attention paid by both newspapers and television to cases she'd been involved with in the past, and law enforcement's use of psychics in general. It was his greatest fear that the killer might have gotten the wind up, gotten scared, gone to ground, or—worst case scenario—moved on, not to be heard from again until someday, in another part of the country, in another city, another town, women began dying.

Wade didn't know how he'd be able to live with himself if he let the sonofabitch get away.

On the other hand, there'd been some progress in the case. The DNA evidence still hadn't come back, which didn't matter much since they didn't yet have a suspect's DNA to compare it to. The canvass of traffic citations was being cross-referenced with juvenile, military and medical records and so far had come up with seven possible suspects. Four of those, known sex offenders, had been brought in for questioning and tentatively ruled out. Three hadn't been located—yet.

Absent some sort of break in the case, the task force was reduced to going back over ground already covered, talking to friends, family, neighbors and coworkers of the victims, sifting through files, culling through databases of similar cases in other cities. There was progress, but it was too slow and too little to suit Wade.

To keep himself from going nuts, he spent some after-hours time—well, okay, some on-the-clock time, as well—looking into the background of one Cory Pearson, journalist.

One thing he had to say. He was who he said he was. There was no dearth of information on him available on the Internet. Wade had been too young at the time to have paid much attention to what was happening on the far side of the world, but it seemed the guy had been a well-known war correspondent in his day—had even been captured and taken prisoner during the Second Gulf War. While a captive in Iraq, he'd met an airman named Tristan Bauer, who had been shot down during the First Gulf War, and at the time had been missing and presumed dead for eight years. They'd both been rescued together—there'd been a big to-do over that, all sorts of medals and honors and receptions at the White House—and in the process, Cory Pearson had met the airman's daughter, Samantha. They hadn't gotten together until years later, though, after the two of them wound up in the same Philippine jungle. Evidently, Pearson had written a book about some of his adventures. That, and a whole bunch of articles for every major news outlet from *Time* magazine to CNN.

Wade was about ready to conclude Tierney must have been mistaken about the source of the emotions she'd picked up that day in the Portland Rose Gardens. He'd probably have chalked the whole thing up to coincidence, except for one thing. With all that information, gazillions of words written by and about the man, there wasn't a thing, not word one about him between his birth—his birth certificate listed his mother as Susan Louise Pearson and his father as Christopher George Pearson and his birthplace as Indianapolis—and when he'd become a journalist. Okay, college. But before that—nada. Which could mean nothing. But could mean something. Sealed juvenile records, maybe? Which he'd need a warrant to access, and he had no cause whatsoever to justify a warrant.

Maybe someday he'd find a way to dig into it a little deeper, but for now...he supposed he could always ask Tierney to try again to pick up something. If he could keep his prurient imagination under control. Which he was having a lot of trouble doing lately.

No, unless another victim turned up, calling Tierney Doyle was simply too damn dangerous.

He thought about her, though. Thought about her a *lot*.

She popped into his head at odd times and in peculiar ways. Driving home from work, seeing a little girl with red-gold curls skipping across the street hanging on to her mother's hand, it occurred to him Tierney would have looked like that when she was little, and if she had a daughter...

Catching a glimpse of a rose, or the scent of one—and roses were everywhere in Portland, in May—always brought her vividly to mind, looking the way she did that day in the gardens, with her shoulders bare and the wind playing with her hair and skirt, and her shoes dangling by their straps from one finger.

He couldn't bite into a hamburger without seeing the blissful smile on her lips as she'd crunched on that veggie sandwich of hers...and remembering the way watching her eat had made hungry juices gather at the back of his throat.

He couldn't look at Officer Williams's crime scene photos without his chest contracting at the vivid recall of Tierney's face when she'd looked at the body, her eyes gone stark with grief and self-blame. And that would lead inevitably to the memory—not so much mental as sensory—of the way she'd felt up against him with his arms wrapped around her and his lips pressed against her hair. The sweet, clean smell of her hair, reminiscent of country roads and moist green gardens in the midst of the ugliness of that day.

Then, of course, there were all the usual ways a beautiful woman occupies a man's mind. Sitting at his desk, looking at the phone and thinking how much he wanted to pick it up and call her. Walking up the stairs to his apartment in the evening, his imagination seeing her nice round bottom swaying back and forth as she mounted the stairs to her place just ahead of him. Waking up in the morning in a sweaty tangle of sheets with the imagined image of her naked body entwined with his fading rapidly from his consciousness, and having to dive into a cold shower to clear his mind so he could get on with his day.

Between Tierney Doyle, Cory Pearson and a stalled murder investigation, Wade wasn't getting a whole lot of sleep. He figured if something didn't break somewhere soon, he might be tempted to do something drastic. Get drunk, or look up an old girlfriend, maybe. Except both of those options had about as much appeal as, say, sharing a lumpy sofa with Bruno the basset hound.

The break finally came on Friday night, though not quite the way he'd expected.

It had been a frustrating week, and as the members of the TK Task Force packed it in, one by one they stopped by Wade's desk to ask if he was planning on joining them for beer and pool at Friendly's, the department's watering hole a couple of blocks up the street. Last to go was Ed Francks, and Wade told him what he'd told the others: he might be along later. He wanted to check something out first.

"Come on, man, give your brain a rest," Ed said as he twirled his jacket off the back of his chair and onto his broad shoulders. "We all need it. This case has us chasin' our tails. Even Superman needs a little R and R now and then, and you ain't no superman."

"This isn't the case." Wade frowned at the screen as he brought up the Google search he'd saved. "Some personal stuff."

He and Francks had been friends for a long time, and partners before that, but the big man wasn't the type to presume. He stood for a moment looking down at Wade, then said quietly, "Anything I can do?"

Wade threw him half a smile and said, "Nah—no biggie. You go on. I might stop by later. Save me a cold one."

"I might, and then again…" Francks grinned, pointed a finger at him to say goodbye, and went off.

As the quiet of the off-hours squad room settled around him, Wade hitched his chair closer to the computer and began a search through his old cases, looking for somebody who *might* be looking for him.

The next time he looked at his watch it was after ten. His head was swimming and he had a cramp between his shoulder blades, and he didn't have any more of an idea who was stalking him—assuming it wasn't Cory Pearson—than when he'd started.

He powered down his computer screen, shoved his chair back and indulged in a good stretch and head scratch. Then he got up, put on his jacket, fished his car keys out of his pocket and turned on his cell phone, tucked his weapon in its holster and headed for the parking garage.

He wasn't sure why, but his nerves were on edge. Maybe looking at all those old cases, thinking about the crimes and the perps he'd helped put away. Thinking even more about the few he hadn't been able to catch, or who had managed to slip through the system's fingers. Grim thoughts, some of them, and plenty of reasons why somebody might feel gleeful about tracking him down. But then again, why would they have to? He was still right here in Portland, Oregon, where the crimes had gone down and the perps were put away. Didn't make sense.

Dark thoughts, perplexing puzzles, flashed through his mind to the rhythm of the echoing scrape of his footsteps on the concrete floor of the parking garage. Not many cars this time of night—night-duty cops, dispatchers, 9-1-1 operators, cleaning crew vans and a few others, like him, working late. He wasn't the jumpy sort; normally, he wouldn't give a thought to the fact that he made a nice clear target walking alone through a deserted garage in the dead of night. Tonight he was conscious of the weight of his weapon nestled against the steady thump of his heartbeat, and his eyes scanned the shadows for suspicious shapes.

He had his car keys in his hand and was about to put them to use when one of those shadows became a flurry of movement on the outer edges of his vision.

In the space of time between two heartbeats he'd whirled and pinned the potential assailant belly-first against the side of his car. He had his weapon in one hand and the assailant's wrist in the other, pulled up and pressed hard between the shoulder blades.

With an adrenaline surge like the crashing of surf inside his head, he barely heard the whimper of pain and the airless, "Wade—please—it's me, Tierney…"

Chapter 7

"Sweet Jesus Lord…"

Wade was slumped against the side of the car with his face in his hands, and Tierney knew from the emotions rolling off of him like thunder that the words weren't meant as blasphemy.

She, on the other hand, was incapable of speech. Incapable of movement of any kind, even to cover her head with her arms, as she instinctively wanted to do. As if that would shield her from the bludgeoning of those emotions

Fury! Fear!

Regret… Remorse… Shame…

Fury again—and something else, something I can't understand because it's so tangled up with everything else.

Wade—please…stop!

"Are you all right?" The question came muffled but

harsh. "Are you…" Then a pause for some muttered swearing. "Did I hurt you?"

She lied…shook her head. And his reply came instantly, almost a snarl.

"Don't do that! Don't lie to me. Of course I hurt you— I was trying to hurt…not *you*—whoever the hell I thought you were. *Damn it,* Doyle! What are you doing here? Were you waiting for me? Why didn't you call me?"

"I tried to." Her voice felt small and timid. "Check your voice mail." She stirred at last, turned and leaned her back against the car next to him, unconsciously mimicking his stance.

There was another long string of swear words, some of which Tierney was sure she'd never heard before. Wade grabbed his cell phone from its holster, thumbed some buttons and glared at the screen.

"I had it turned off. I was working on…something," he said in a calmer voice, transferring the glare to her. "But you could have said something, called out— Jeez, girl, give a guy some warning. I'm in the middle of a murder investigation, there's a serial killer running loose, and I've got God knows who stalking me, maybe. It's a miracle I didn't—" He broke off to stare at her. "Hell. Are you *crying?*"

"No," she said, and dashed the betraying tear from her cheek. The last thing she needed tonight was for him to put his arms around her again. As far as self-control went, she figured that would just about do hers in completely.

Which evidently he realized, because instead of reaching for her, he folded his arms on his chest as if to keep himself from doing so and frowned at her. "Look, I'm sorry, okay? And you didn't answer my question. Why are you here? Did something happen—" He straightened, then leaned toward her, suddenly on full alert. "Did you pick up something new on our killer? My stalker?"

She shook her head and sniffed, swiped at another tear, then said in a choked voice, "Nothing like that. I probably shouldn't have bothered you with it. I didn't know who else—"

"Damn it, Miss Tee—"

"It's my grandmother, Wade. She's gone. I've looked all over for her. I can't find her anywhere, and I don't know what to do. She's out there somewhere and—" Her voice caught on a little sob of grief and terror.

What could he do? He'd tried to keep his hands off of her, truly he had. But he was the comforter, the one weeping women counted on, and if she'd been any other woman…oh, what the hell.

He snaked one arm out and hooked it around her shoulders and brought her into the curve of his arm. Then that seemed like a half-assed kind of way to comfort her, and anyway, who was he kidding? He had no doubt *she* already knew where this was heading. So he turned her and got her properly wrapped in his arms with her head tucked in under his chin and her body snug and warm against his. Then he closed his eyes and let out a sigh while he gently rocked her.

After a while he lifted his head and said softly, "Tell me what happened, Miss Tee."

She pulled away from him, wiping at her eyes with both hands, and he had the good sense to let her go.

"I know I should have called the police right away instead of trying to find her myself, and then waiting for you, but it was after hours, and I would have had to call

9-1-1, and my name's been in the news so much lately, and I was afraid some reporter might pick it up—".

"Never mind that. How long has she been missing?"

"I don't know. I don't even know what time it is now. I'd been in the studio, painting, and it was later than usual when I went upstairs. Jeannette was asleep in her chair in front of the television. So I thought it would be safe to take a shower before fixing her dinner. I don't know what happened. I was tired…maybe I forgot to lock the dead bolt. It couldn't have been more than ten minutes, Wade. And when I came out she was *gone.*"

By this time Wade had his car unlocked and was guiding Tierney around to the passenger side door. Oblivious, she went on talking while he settled her in and fastened her seat belt for her.

"The front door was open, and she wasn't anywhere— not in the gallery or even on the street. I think I sort of went to pieces at that point. I know I went running off down the street like a crazy person, looking for her, calling and calling. Finally I realized I couldn't cover enough ground that way, and since I didn't even know which way she'd gone… Anyway, at some point I started thinking rationally—sort of—and went back and got my car. I've been driving around, calling your cell phone for…I don't know how long. Oh, Wade—"

She was looking up at him with swimming eyes when he bent down and kissed her.

Not a long kiss. Just a short, sweet one. Very sweet, although her lips tasted of salt and tears. He felt a peculiar little contraction around his heart as he pushed back from her and gently closed the door.

When he had the car running and almost ready to pull out onto the street, he looked over at Tierney, who was sitting exactly as he'd left her after the kiss. "Hey," he said, and she swiveled her head toward him, looking dazed. His heart gave another of those funny kicks as he wondered for a moment whether he'd gone too far, crossed some kind of line with her. He sure hoped not. Because he knew suddenly that he'd be losing something of real importance if he had.

Then she smiled. Just that. And he knew he *had* crossed a line—a different one—and that it was both a good and a scary thing. And that, either way, there was no going back now.

"Hmm?" she said, and he had to think for a moment what it was he'd wanted to ask her.

"I was just wondering," he said as it came to him, "about your…*thing*. Your gift. You said your grandmother has it, too. You can't—I don't know…tune in, pick up on her— wherever she is?"

"I used to be able to. Not anymore." The sadness in her voice made his throat ache. "The connection between us used to be like a river, this broad, deep stream of feeling, only unlike a river, it flowed both ways. This past year it's been slowly drying up, until now it's only this little trickle. Once in a while something comes through, but most of the time…" She shook her head and finished in a whisper. "No…I can't hear her now."

"I'm sorry."

He drove now as he often did, she'd noticed, when he was moved, or emotional about something: with his window down, elbow on the sill and his hand over his mouth. But the emotions, whatever they were, were shielded from her.

Her lips, where he'd kissed her, felt cold, and she touched them with her fingertips to warm them.

"Jeannette is the only family I've ever known," she said softly.

"You told me about your mother—she left when you were three, right?" He glanced at her as she nodded. "Kind of a lousy thing to do to a kid."

"I suppose so…although I've never been angry with her about it. Partly because I was able to empathize with her, thanks to Gran's connection. Neither of us blamed my mother. I know Gran didn't. She blamed herself."

"How so?"

"Well…to understand that I think you'd have to have known Jeannette the way she was back then. She was so beautiful, so full of life—a young Maureen O'Hara, people said. And in Hollywood in those days, that was saying something."

"Hollywood?"

"Yes—that's where she lived then."

"You're kidding."

"No, seriously. It's where my mother grew up. I was born there."

"I thought your grandmother was Irish—old country Irish, I mean."

"Oh, she is. Definitely. She moved to the United States after my grandfather was killed—her *husband,* I just found out," she added with some chagrin, still feeling hurt that her grandmother had kept such an important part of her history from her. "I always thought she was a single mother—it did seem to run in our family—and that she'd left Ireland to avoid the shame of an out-of-wedlock baby.

Not so, apparently. She was married after all, and her husband's name was Tommy. He died fighting the British in Northern Ireland.

"Anyway—where was I? Oh yes…my mother. Isabella. I suspect it's not easy being the daughter of a beautiful mother."

"So…your mother wasn't? Beautiful, I mean."

"Oh, she was. From the photos I've seen of her, she was a very pretty woman. But I'm sure she went through awkward stages, and by the time she was in her teens, she had a definite self-image problem. Compared to Jeannette, Izzy didn't *feel* pretty. She lacked the sparkle, the vivacious personality that made my grandmother light up a whole room—wherever she went, every eye would be on her. Poor Izzy…"

Wade glanced at her, then back at the street ahead, his smile wry. "I think I can guess the rest. She's ripe for the first guy that comes along who pays attention to her instead of her mother. He tells her she's pretty, and next thing you know, she's pregnant. And he, being the kind of guy who tells a woman whatever it takes to get her into bed, is long gone by the time you make your appearance." He paused, frowning. "Sad old story, but it sure as hell doesn't justify abandoning her kid."

"Ah," said Tierney softly, "but you're forgetting the worst part. *The Gift.*"

Another quick glance. "She had it, too? Your mother?"

"No—that was the problem. She didn't. So, Izzy's cursed with a mother who's not only a great beauty, but a psychic on top of it. It must have been just awful for her. And then, when her own child started showing signs…"

"At *three?* Isn't that kind of young to be doing... whatever it is you do?"

"Oh, I was much younger than that, probably. I think by the time I was three she had gotten to the point where she'd had enough of it."

"And you haven't seen or heard from her since?"

Tierney shook her head. "I like to think she found someone...someone she could be happy with. I always imagine her that way—happy."

"You ever miss her? When you were a kid, I mean." His voice was unexpectedly gruff, and she looked at him for a long moment before she replied.

"I don't remember missing her. I was always closer to my grandmother, even before my mother left. That's what's so sad. And why I'm not angry with her for going. Why Jeannette and I...we've always blamed ourselves rather than her."

He didn't answer, and his profile was hard to read in the changing light of the streetlamps they passed. She wanted to know whether he understood...whether he judged. But she couldn't *feel* him. Knowing she shouldn't, she reached out to him with her mind...probing his shields. Just for a moment.

What she felt made her gasp.

He threw her a look and said, "What?"

She shook her head and said, "Nothing." And was glad of the dim light that would hide the flush she felt flooding her cheeks, her face. Her whole body.

"Miss Tee," he said softly, "don't do that." And then he melted her heart by adding, "Please."

She gazed straight ahead while the tears pooled—she

dared not blink. "I don't think I can describe it," she whispered. "I've never felt anything like it before."

"Where did it come from—this thing you *felt?*" She didn't have to look at him to know he was frowning.

"I don't know," she said, lying.

"Your grandmother? My stalker? Have anything to do with our case?"

"No…" She turned to look over her shoulder, realizing they were on her street.

Wade turned sharply, pulled into an empty parking spot and stopped.

"We're going to tackle this logically," he said, shifting in the seat to face her. "Look, I doubt your grandmother just wandered around the apartment until she accidently happened to end up outside. Especially since you said it happened quickly. She must have thought she was going somewhere. In her mind she had a purpose, some reason she felt she needed to leave. Maybe she thought she was going…I don't know, grocery shopping? Is there someplace nearby she might have been accustomed to going before she got sick, someplace she'd go on foot, maybe?"

"Her hairdresser," Tierney said slowly, staring at him. "Her salon used to be just up the street—about four blocks from here. Jeannette had a standing appointment for a wash and set every Friday. For years."

Wade shrugged. "Today's Friday."

"Yes, but I don't see—she doesn't have any idea what day it is. Except—"

"Except…what?"

"Every once in a while she'll have a moment—it's kind of like a shaft of sunlight breaking through on a cloudy day, you know? A moment of lucidity. It never lasts very long, but…oh, Wade." The tears spilled over again and she wiped at them without much effect. "What if she did? The salon isn't even there anymore. I think it's a flower shop now. And that late it would have been closed anyway. Oh, poor Jennie…" She covered her mouth with her hand to smother a shuddering sob.

Wade was already pulling back onto the street. "We'll find her," he said gruffly. "Hang in there, sweetheart."

She nodded, sniffed, and wasn't surprised when Wade handed her his handkerchief. She'd understood the endearment, too, understood it was just his nature to comfort and protect. She wondered if it was something he'd been born with, or if he'd learned from the person—whoever it was— who'd comforted and protected him as a child…the one in his dreams.

"There—that's it. That's where her hairdresser used to be." Tierney sat up and twisted around to look as they cruised past the florist's shop that had once been a beauty salon. Then, as she sank back in disappointment, "I don't see her. It was too much to hope for, I suppose. Oh, poor Gran." Her voice broke and she finished in a whisper. "She must have been so confused."

Wade was cruising slowly, now, while they both scanned the shadows in doorways and between parked cars for anything that might have been a huddled human form. A block or so farther on he turned right and they found themselves in a residential neighborhood surrounding a city park. He slowed the car to a crawl.

"That park up there. Did you check it out?"

She nodded and replied in a choked voice. "Several times."

"Once more won't hurt." He pulled the car into a vacant space beside a fire hydrant and stopped. They both got out and hurried across the street at a half run.

"It's late," Wade said. "She's probably tired. I'm thinking she's curled up sound asleep somewhere."

"We could probably cover more ground if we split up," Tierney said. Her voice sounded small and scared.

He didn't reply, just reached for her hand and wrapped his around it. Gave it a gentle squeeze. He could feel her look at him, but he didn't look back at her. His chest already felt a couple of sizes too small for what was going on inside him.

A man passed them, walking a dog—a terrier of some kind—moving quickly and purposefully. He acknowledged them with a brief nod. Wade could hear the whap and bop of balls from the lighted tennis courts nearby, and whoops and jeers from some kids shooting hoops out of sight beyond the restrooms. A nice night, he thought, watching moths swirl and dance in the mercury lights. Peaceful…wholesome…safe.

A nice night to be out walking, holding hands with a beautiful woman.

Somewhere in this night a confused old woman is wandering…lost. And a killer might be stalking his next victim.

The hand nestled in his jerked suddenly. Gripped hard, then tugged free.

"There she is." It was half gasp and half sob. And Tierney was running across the grass. Dropping to her knees beside a park bench where a huddled figure sat muttering to herself and rocking…rocking…rocking.

When Wade got there moments later, Jeannette lifted her

smudged and tear-streaked face, wiped a hand across one cheek and smiled at him—her radiant and youthful smile.

"I know you," she crowed in delight. Then she turned to her granddaughter with a look of heartrending bewilderment. "I do...don't I? I think...I must..."

"Yes, of course you do," Tierney said tenderly. "Come, love—let's go home now."

It was after midnight when Wade heard a door somewhere down the short hallway close softly. At the sound of light footsteps he picked up the remote, turned down the volume on the TV and shifted on the couch to watch Tierney as she came into the living room.

She joined him on the couch, one leg tucked under her so she was facing him. He could see she'd been crying, although she did her best to hide it with a look of surprise and a smile.

"You didn't have to stay."

He ignored that. "How is she?"

"Sleeping. She was worn out, poor thing." She raked her fingers through her curls, looked around for distraction and settled for "What're you watching?".

He shrugged. "All-night poker."

She cut her eyes at him. "Couldn't find anything more exciting?"

"What, you don't think we've had enough excitement for one night?"

Then he added, "Actually, this is pretty exciting. They're down to the final three and one guy just went 'all in.'"

She laughed, and a tear rolled down her cheek. She brushed at it with a furious gesture. "I don't know what's the matter with me. I haven't cried before. Not over this."

"Maybe you needed to."

She clapped a hand over her eyes, but below it her mouth looked blurred and vulnerable. He saw her lips quiver in spite of her valiant efforts to control them. "I've lost her, Wade," she whispered. "The Jeannette Doyle I love so much—my grandmother...my gran—she's just... gone."

His throat felt swollen and scratchy, so his voice came out harsher than he intended. "Look, you've lost a loved one. Why are you trying so hard not to grieve?"

She didn't reply, only drew a shuddering breath and added the other hand to the one already covering her eyes.

He saw there was no use fighting it. So he reached for her, then leaned back against the corner of the couch and pulled her toward him. When he had her nicely tucked in against his chest and was fairly sure she wasn't going anywhere, he picked up the remote and muted the TV. Then he settled down to hold her and stroke her hair while she sobbed like a heartbroken child.

Little by little the sobs quieted...became fitful shudders and hiccuping gulps, desperate sniffs and poignant whimpers...and finally the slightly stuffy but even breathing that meant she'd fallen asleep. Wade tucked in his chin and looked down at her to make sure, then settled her more comfortably and stared at the silently flickering TV screen.

The beginning of awareness came suddenly to Tierney, and with it a state of confused paralysis. She lay absolutely still and tried to take stock.

Where am I? Why is the pillow moving? What's that sound? What time is it?

She identified the sound first. Snoring. Gran snored sometimes, but this wasn't Gran.

Ah—she remembered. This was Wade. She was on the couch, lying cradled in Wade's arms. He'd held her, she recalled, while she cried. She must have cried herself to sleep. He was snoring softly now, and since her head was pillowed on his chest, each deep breath moved it up and down. She opened her eyes but still didn't know what time it was. There was an old black-and-white rerun of a Cassius Clay boxing match playing on the muted TV.

She lifted her head, held her breath and attempted to extricate herself from Wade's embrace without waking him. She should have known better than to try.

Naturally, as soon as her body began to stir, so did his. His arms tightened around her and his body shifted in subtle ways that somehow made it all the easier for hers to conform to the shape of his. She felt his hands move on her back, glide downward in a slow but purposeful way as if they knew exactly where they were going.

I should wake him…can't let him do this. He's only doing this because he's asleep, mostly…doesn't really know what he's doing…he'll be embarrassed when he realizes…

But it feels so good. It's been a long time since anyone's touched me like this.

She began to respond. Knew she shouldn't…but, oh…it just seemed impossible not to. Her body moved of its own accord, sinuously, catlike, to the rhythm of his stroking. The cadence of her breathing quickened. She slid her hand down his side and felt his do the same on hers.

She knew she had no intention of stopping.

He drew a deep, shuddering breath. An awakening

breath, as his hard, bristly chin nudged her forehead. Asked…urged…demanded.

Blindly obedient, she lifted her face as he asked—searching. Felt his body tense and tighten under her as he raised his head…then a breath-stopping surge of passion as two hungry mouths found each other. The passion rolled over her like a sea wave…engulfed her. It came from inside her and from outside, too—from him.

Just that—she felt no other emotions, just lust. And her own equaled his.

I need this so much…

It was like a drug she'd been craving. A drug she'd been denied for too long.

He eased one knee between her legs and slowly raised it, putting pressure on the nerve-rich places between, and at the same time his hands skimmed upward and found their way under her blouse. His rough hands on her bare skin felt so good she whimpered, a pitifully grateful sound.

His searching fingers found the fastening of her bra and unhooked it, and she obligingly raised her torso and lifted her arms so he could pull both blouse and bra over her head. Like a prisoner released from bondage, she gave a throaty little chuckle of pleasure. He answered with a whisper of approving laughter. His fingers spread wide across her rib cage, then slipped to her sides, thumbs stroking the undersides of her breasts as with strong hands and hard-muscled thigh he lifted her up so that her bared breasts were his for the taking.

And take them he did…each nipple, already sensitized to the point of pain, he first nipped and tongued to intolerable hardness, then sucked deep in a way that tugged and tormented places deep, deep inside her body. She put her head back, wanting to scream, helpless with desire, caught between his imprisoning thigh and his tormenting mouth.

Did she want him to stop, or fear that he would?

Dimly, she felt his hands probing, seeking a way under the waistband of her jeans. Trembling now, she lifted herself higher to allow him better access, and almost sobbed with relief when she felt the buttons and zipper give way to his impatient fingers. Brain-fogged by passion already, she didn't give a thought to the strength and skill it took for him to roll them both onto their sides, remembering to shift so as not to tumble them off the couch while he tugged her jeans and underpants down past her hips. Quickly, she kicked them off, then reached greedily for his belt.

She knew there was no longer any question of anyone being half asleep—there could be no excuse on that account. Both were fully aware, completely and purposefully engaged. But for some reason, neither spoke. She didn't look into his eyes, either. She opened hers only to watch her hands as they struggled to dispose of the barrier of his clothes.

Meanwhile, *his* hands, not being handicapped by such obstacles, were having their way with her. Stroking her buttocks, the cleft between, the backs of her thighs, finding every swelling, aching, nerve-abundant spot, some she'd never dreamed could hold so much sensation, so much pleasure.

Thus distracted, she wasn't sure how she got his shirt open but somehow did. With a joyful little gasp she went exploring now, herself, using lips and tongue and teeth and fingertips…senses of smell, taste and touch, learning his body's unique scents, flavors, textures…crispness of hair, salty-slick glazing of sweat over smooth warm skin, the giving hardness of muscle beneath…the intriguing anomalies of hardened nipples and ropy scars.

Intriguing for a moment, but…not enough. She needed more.

The need was assuaged, but only partly, when his mouth took hers again. Lost in his mouth, all but overwhelmed with the kiss, still she whimpered deep in her throat with the frustration of trying to get his belt unbuckled and his pants removed—hard to do without separating from him. And she couldn't bear to be separated from him, even for that long.

Impossible…

Without any words being spoken, somehow he seemed to know. Without breaking the kiss, he slipped his hands between their bodies, unzipped his pants and jerked them down—not all the way, just far enough. Swiftly, then, he pulled her legs apart and twisted his body so she was once again on top of him, and she chuckled with pleasure at the feel of him, smooth and hot and hard against her belly.

Then…he drew her knees up along his sides, stroked his hands inward over the backs of her thighs and gripped her firmly. And held her wide open to him and pushed into her.

She cried out—couldn't help it. It had been a long time for her. When he hesitated she kissed him hungrily, whimpering not with pain but with the urgency of her need, wordlessly begging him not to stop. And once again he seemed to know what she needed without a word being spoken.

Murmuring assurances, he held her hips tightly and raised her just enough so he could withdraw—only a little—and before she could reach for another breath to protest, brought her down again. This time he ignored her body's resistance, brought her hips hard against his and thrust deep. Lifted her again...then set himself so deeply inside her she cried out again and arched her back, gasping for breath.

No misreading her this time. He didn't withdraw even a tiny bit, but half raised his upper body, wrapped his arms around her and buried his face in the hollow of her throat, absorbing her thrusts as she drove herself against him again and again, urging him deeper inside her than seemed possible. And she was aching inside but oblivious to everything except a terrible, all-consuming passion. Passion unlike anything she'd ever felt before.

Then...as she felt the building heat and pressure of his climax, her passion became panic. He tried to soothe her with his wordless growls and murmurs of reassurance, even as his body hardened and his muscles contracted beneath her hands and between her legs. And as he uttered a deep-throated groan and emptied himself into her, she sobbed with the pain of intolerable frustration, because her own release remained just out of reach.

But instead of collapsing into an inert heap, as men in her admittedly limited experience customarily did at such moments, Wade lifted his head from the cushions, gathered her hair in one hand and brought her mouth to his, slowly and deliberately reclaimed it, nibbling and biting her swollen, sensitized lips while he carefully rolled her onto her back. Then, leaning down to her he released her hair but deepened the kiss, as with his hands he pulled her legs wide apart...held her hips firmly to keep her still while with his thumbs he gently stroked and teased her most sensitive places.

She'd never experienced anything like it before, never known her body capable of such sensations. The urge to move, the compulsion to squirm, to writhe—not knowing whether to escape the torment or to beg for more—was terrible. But he was ruthless, holding her motionless as he slowed his stroke…withdrawing, tantalizing, teasing… then finally sliding deep inside her, only to withdraw again…rocking her slower, yet slower, and even slower still. Until she felt as though her body would surely burst with the pressure of so much feeling.

So much…too much!

And she sobbed and sobbed until, with a wild, keening cry, she finally shattered, utterly devastated…came to earth trembling and dazed, almost in shock.

Wade gathered her as close as he could without risk of crushing her, and held her, rocked her, tenderly cradled her face in the hollow of his neck while he caressed her hair and wiped the tears from her cheeks. He didn't try to speak, knowing he was probably in no shape to do so with any coherence anyway, being pretty overwhelmed and shaky himself.

It was only after Tierney had stopped trembling and *his* heart rate and breathing had returned to something approaching normal that he cleared his throat and inquired with utter seriousness, "So, do I have The Gift to thank for that?"

Chapter 8

He felt the ripples of her laughter with the supersensitive part of himself still nestled inside her.

"Wow," he said, although it came out more like something between a growl and a purr. "That's a very interesting sensation."

"What is?"

He nudged her head with his chin...ran his hand lightly over her back. "You. Laughing. I can feel it inside you."

"Gee, I'd think you'd be—"

"I know you would, but you'd be wrong." He stopped caressing her and sucked in a breath. "Good God. Is it possible it's catching—this gift of yours?"

She tilted her head and smiled up at him, lashes half veiling her eyes and lips looking blurred and soft. "I told you, what I have isn't that unusual. It's mostly a matter of degree."

"Hmm," he said, thinking about it. "Maybe." A little shiver ran through him, though he realized it was more mental than physical. He'd never been so conscious of the workings of his own mind. Thoughts, yeah—he usually tried to stay on top of those. It was the feelings, the reactions, the stuff that popped into his mind whether he wanted it to or not that he was starting to be aware of, and wonder about. Right now he was pretty sure he had his fire walls up—blocking, she called it—even if he didn't have a clue *how* he did it. And it was pretty obvious he hadn't been a little while ago.

"That was a serious question, by the way," he said after a moment. "Did the fact that you were picking up my…you know…" Lord, what *would* he call it? Ardor? Passion? Pure unadulterated lust?

Actually, *that* he had no problem with. It was the stuff that might have leaked along with it that worried him. Those were things he hadn't had time to sort out himself, and he was pretty certain he'd need to do some serious editing before sharing them with anyone—particularly *her.*

"I'm not sure," Tierney said, tucking her face back under his chin where he couldn't see it. It felt warm, though, and he wondered if she could possibly be blushing. "I've never had it happen before—not like that."

"Come on." Oh, but a part of him wanted to grin from ear to ear with the purely involuntary swelling of his masculine pride. Then he said wryly, "Well, I wish I thought my—ahem—lovemaking skills had something to do with it, but it's more reasonable to assume you were picking up on my—ahem—enthusiasm."

Up popped her head again. This time she kissed him—and not lightly. "Stop trying to find reasons," she murmured as she closed her eyes, licked her lips, then opened them again to glare at him. "There was nothing even remotely reasonable about what just happened to us."

Wade cupped her head with his hand and brought her mouth back to his. It was a long time before he released her enough to ask, "Feel like being unreasonable some more?"

Tierney gulped air and managed to produce sound—a whisper. "Okay…except…well, there are a couple of small things…"

"Yeah?" said Wade in a deep, guttural voice, nibbling at her soft, swollen lips. "Like what?"

"I'd like very much to see you naked."

"Glad to oblige." He was laughing. She could feel him laughing, growing hard inside her. "What else?"

"Oh—" She grew breathless, riding his gentle rocking like a boat on a lazy swell. "You're right, that is an interesting…"

He stopped her with a harder, deeper kiss as he continued to move slowly, sinuously inside her, then said, "What else? Time for talk is just about over."

He was right; she was finding it harder and harder to breathe, much less talk. "Well…under the circumstances, this is probably moot, but—"

"Oh, hell." He went completely still and closed his eyes. "I forgot to use—"

Now it was she who stopped him with a kiss. "Shh—*we* forgot." She felt only a moment's guilt at the almost certain knowledge that it wouldn't have mattered to her back then if she *had* remembered. "I'm on the pill, so that's covered. And I'm very healthy…"

"So'm I, but that's—anyway, I don't have anything with me. Do you?"

"No," she said, laughing softly, teasing him with a little body wiggle, "but as I said, it's kind of pointless to worry about it now…isn't it?"

"Yeah…" There was that growl again, as he moved into her in a testing way. "So…anything else you wanted to discuss while we're being…uh, reasonable?"

"Well, if we…managed to do what we did…on this awful couch, imagine what we could accomplish in my nice roomy bed."

He paused, lying still but letting his hands wander at will over her back and bottom while he considered the options: withdraw from her and move to a more comfortable venue, with all its limitless possibilities…or stay where he was. "Do you really want me to stop?" he asked weakly.

Tierney's only reply was a moan. He kissed her throat as he resumed his slow movements both inside and outside her body. Murmured against her thumping pulse, "How about a compromise?"

"Okay…" Her voice had grown high and airless. She'd have said the same thing if he'd asked her to consider flying to the moon.

"Stay with me now…"

She felt herself being lifted, his strong arms taking her with him as he knelt on the sofa cushions. Then her legs were astride his hips and his arms under her bottom supported her weight. She laced her arms around his neck, buried her face in the hollow of his shoulder and gave a giddy little cry as he rose to his feet.

"Lord, I'm glad you're strong," she whispered, laughing, dizzy and utterly helpless now.

Wade was too busy disposing of his pants to reply. They

fell to the floor at last, and he kicked them out of the way. From somewhere off in the distance he heard Tierney give a pleased little chuckle as she peeled off his shirt, and then her strong fingers were kneading his bare back and buttocks and her soft body was an all-over caress as she swayed and writhed against him. He lost track of his legs.

"Uh…babe," he said weakly, "my plan was to carry you to your bedroom like this, but I don't think I'm going to make it. Plan B…comin' up." He sank with her onto the arm of the couch and pulled her legs snugly around him. "How's that?"

She couldn't answer him. The penetration was so deep, deeper than she'd thought possible. Her slightest movement set off rockets of sensation deep inside…and yet the velvety caress of his belly sliding over hers, the crisp tingle of chest hair teasing her nipples, the gentle but inexorable pressure of his hands…nimble, clever fingers… were impossible to resist. She couldn't help it…rocked harder against him, and heat and pressure forced a cry from her throat, something deep-throated and primitive she'd never heard herself utter before. She rocked again, and lost sensation in her feet—except at the same time every inch of her skin seemed on fire.

She wanted to scream…gripped Wade's shoulders, arched her back and bit her lip to keep those terrible cries inside. She wanted the pressure and sensation to stop—at least her mind did. Her mind was sobbing, sobbing. *I can't… I can't…*

But her body wouldn't listen. Her body only wanted more. Wanted more of *him*.

He knew the desperate struggle going on inside her, felt

it in the tenseness of her muscles, the way her torso writhed and shuddered in his arms, heard it in her whimpering breaths. Wanting only to ease her distress, he left one arm across her lower body to guide her as she rocked against him and brought the other to cradle her head. He whispered, "Shh…" as he pressed the side of her face to his, and felt a slick warmth on his cheek he knew must be her tears.

Though almost overwhelmed with tenderness for her, in the masculine way, of course, he didn't breathe a word of what was going on inside of him.

Sweetheart…it's okay. Don't fight it, my dearest…trust me. Let me take you with me. It's okay… I'm here and I'm holding you… I won't let anything hurt you. It will be all right, I promise. Come with me, my love…

The feelings were inside her, filling her like a rising flood. She didn't question or wonder about them, but clutched at them the way a wild animal, drowning, will grab hold of just about anything, even the hand of a human being, its mortal enemy. She wrapped the feelings around her like a cloak and felt joy flood her whole being, like sunlight. Laughing, she lifted her face to its warmth and thought, *This is what love feels like.*

Wade felt the easing in her muscles, heard the soft ripples of her laughter, and felt his whole body swell with purely masculine exaltation. He felt great and powerful, a man among men, able not only to give his woman unimaginable pleasure, but to protect and care for her, as well. He felt almost godlike, so tuned to the workings of this woman's body that he knew exactly when she was on the brink of climax, and so confident in his power and skill that he could ease her back from the edge, yet not lose the crescendo or send her crashing once more into panic. And all without saying a word.

Stay with me, sweetheart. Not yet...not yet. Let's ride this wave together...a while longer...a little more. Stay with me, love...

And so she did.

She'd never imagined she could obey a man so implicitly. Of course, she could obey him because at this moment she trusted him, absolutely and completely. And trusted him because she knew his feelings. *At this moment, at least, I know them...*

It was probably both simpler and more complicated than that, and she certainly didn't pause to reason it out then. She was operating on pure instinct and raw emotion, both almost unheard of for her—though she didn't think of that, either, until much later.

Now, love? Will you take this ride with me? Don't be afraid... I'm right here, holding you... I'll keep you safe. Are you ready to let go now?

He heard her answer in her gasping cry, "Yes...please, *yes!*" Felt it in the quakings and clenchings that began deep inside her and built to a cataclysm that claimed every part of her body. But by then he was involved with cataclysms of his own, and no longer sure he was as mighty and all-powerful as he'd thought he was. He was terribly grateful for her arms around him, and her fingers digging into his muscles and her strong, slender body in his arms for him to hold on to while his own went pretty much out of his control.

It was afterward, utterly drained and weak as a newborn calf, that Wade had his own moment of panic. It came when he realized he'd completely forgotten to block.

* * *

They never did make it to Tierney's bedroom—not that night. For both of them, for nerves so overtaxed and muscles so spent, the journey of a few yards seemed like a thousand miles.

By slow degrees they managed to move themselves into a reasonably comfortable tangle on the couch, with various unidentified articles of clothing making do for towels and a soft afghan throw—and each other—as covers.

In the last moments of consciousness, Wade mumbled an inquiry—a single word.

"Jeannette?"

Tierney murmured, "She'll sleep late…" And tumbled into oblivion.

Although there hadn't been much left of the night when they'd gone to sleep, Tierney woke at her usual time—partly due to predictable bodily needs and discomforts, she was sure. Leaving Wade snoring peacefully on the couch, she crept off to check on Jeannette—still sound asleep—and then to the bathroom, where she gave the bathtub a longing glance before turning on the shower instead. As nice as it would have been to soak away some of those discomforts she'd awakened with, she didn't trust her hot water supply to last through both a full tub and the shower Wade would surely be wanting when he woke up. And Jeannette was going to need bathing after her evening's adventures, too.

Only when she was standing in the shower with her eyes closed, lovely hot water beating down on her scalp and sluicing over the tender places elsewhere on her body, did she finally let herself think.

Wade.

She opened the door carefully, just a crack at first, like someone unlocking a forbidden vault, nervous about what she would find inside.

He forgot to block.

But she wouldn't be reading too much into the emotions he'd allowed past his barricades last night…earlier this morning. Tierney was a realist; being privy to people's most private and innermost feelings made it pretty much impossible for her not to be.

Not that she thought Wade's emotions weren't real. The beauty of emotions was that they couldn't lie. However, they could be, and often were, fleeting. In the throes of some pretty great sex—and it had been *truly* awesome; she couldn't repress a smile and some shivers just thinking about it—a man might easily believe himself to be in love with the person who'd provided him with it. Anyone could—something *she'd* do well to remember—but mostly men. Because, as she was in a unique position to know, men tended to fall in love with the woman they were having great sex with, while women had great sex with the man they were in love with.

So how does that explain what happened to me last night?

It was a question that was obviously going to require a lot more thought, but she'd used more than her share of the hot water already. And the rhythmic thumping she could hear even with the water running meant Gran was awake, and that Wade, if he wasn't already, probably would be very soon.

Wade.

Her insides clenched and her breathing faltered as memories washed over her. She felt as if she'd been caught up in a flood of melted…oh, something warm and sweet and gooey…and she didn't need to be thinking such thoughts, not with Wade out there in the living room and Jeannette pounding on the door of her room demanding to be let out.

She braced herself and turned the shower to cold, and made herself stand under the spray, gasping, until she was covered from head to toe in goose bumps. She thought of it as penance.

Wade had been awake since shortly *before* Tierney disentangled herself from him and crept away to the bathroom. Though desperately in need of that convenience himself, he hadn't quite felt up to the gymnastics involved in levering himself out of the couch cushions and climbing over a sweetly slumbering woman in order to make use of it. Now he waited until he heard the shower running, then got up, sorted out his pants and pulled them on, then padded barefoot and shirtless to the kitchen to look for coffee.

When Jeannette started pounding on her bedroom door, he considered whether he should go and let her out. Problem was, he doubted she'd remember who he was, and he thought it might be upsetting to the lady to have her door opened by a large bare-chested male stranger.

Or, considering this *particular* lady, it might not. Either way, he decided to let Tierney handle it.

Once the coffeemaker had burped out enough to fill a cup, he poured one for himself and sat down at the table to think about how this was going to go and what he should do about it. However, it didn't take him long to realize there wasn't much he could conclude about the situation without the other person involved being present and, hopefully, contributing her two cents' worth.

Just seeing her, watching her eyes when she walked into her kitchen and found him sitting at her table drinking her coffee on this "morning after"—that was going to tell him a lot, right there.

His nerves kicked involuntarily when he heard a door open somewhere down the hallway, and then another. He sat calmly, sipping hot coffee and telling himself his heart wasn't beating faster, and listened to the sound of voices— hers, soft and sweet and soothing, and Jeannette's, high and querulous and complaining—and footsteps going here and there, drawers opening and closing. Footsteps again, dying as they crossed the living room rug.

He told himself he wasn't even a wee bit disappointed when it was Jeannette, not Tierney, who wandered into the kitchen, looking freshly scrubbed and remarkably serene after her ordeal. Her hair was brushed and hanging loose on her shoulders like a young girl's, and she wore a flowing caftan in peacock colors that almost matched her eyes.

It must be one of the perks of Alzheimer's, Wade thought, that she'd have no recollection of being lost and scared and all alone in a big city at night.

She hesitated only a moment when she saw him sitting there, then gave him a scrutinizing stare as she came closer. She offered him one white-dove hand and said briskly, "Well, as you've probably deduced, I am Isabella's mother." The hand nested in his for only a moment, then flitted off in a blithe little wave. "Oh, don't look so alarmed, dear boy, I'm not going to bring out the shotgun. Izzy's a grown woman, you know. She's free to sleep with whomever she pleases."

Wade hastily gulped back whatever it was he'd planned to say as Jeannette shuffled off in the direction of the refrigerator. Halfway there, though, she halted, and a panicky frown pleated her forehead. "I made some coffee," he said gently. "Would you care for some?"

She hesitated for a moment, then turned back to him, eyebrows arched and lips curved in a smile of aching sweetness. Now when she spoke it was in the thick Irish brogue.

"Fer shame, Tommy-me-darlin'. Havin' your little joke, I suppose, since ye know good-n'well how I love me tea in the mornin'..." And she bent down and planted a kiss on the top of Wade's head.

He was saved from having to think how to reply to that by a blessed sound.

"Now, Gran, you know that's not Tommy. Tommy died, remember? A long time ago." Tierney put an arm around her grandmother's waist and gently but firmly guided her to a chair.

Jeannette peered up at her in bewilderment as she sank slowly into the chair, that heart-tugging smile only a memory. "Izzy?"

"No, darling, it's Tee. And this nice man is Wade Callahan—you met him, remember?" She threw Wade a look and winked, and his breathing stumbled.

She was wearing jeans and a yellow T-shirt with a chain of daisies embroidered along the scooped neckline. Her cheeks were flushed and her damp hair had been caught up in a ponytail, the shorter curls already escaping. For the first time in a long while he thought of cheerleaders.

If he hadn't known better, based on some nagging bodily discomforts, he'd have been tempted to suspect the whole night had been some sort of wild erotic fantasy. A wet dream. On steroids.

Lord help him, at least that thought he did remember to block.

Tierney said, "You made coffee? Thank you." Her smile was like an accolade. He felt as if he'd just been knighted by the queen. "Are you hungry?"

"Like a wolf," he growled, belatedly hoping she'd miss—or at least ignore—the double meaning.

He sat, sipping but not tasting his coffee, and watched her while she fixed Jeannette instant oatmeal with brown sugar and butter, then got out a bowl and a box of Cheerios for herself. She offered to make him something—eggs, French toast, maybe?—but he managed to mumble something to the effect that the Cheerios would be fine. It had been a long time since he'd eaten Cheerios for breakfast.

It was while he was shoveling in spoonfuls of milk and a kids' cereal, listening to an old lady crooning contentedly to her own breakfast, and smiling across the table at the woman with whom he'd just enjoyed the most passionate night of his life, that it came to Wade: he was happy. At that moment, happier than he could remember being in a very long time. Maybe his whole life.

About the time Wade was chasing down the last floating Cheerio, Jeannette got up from the table and wandered off, having forgotten, he assumed, about the remaining half of her breakfast. Resisting the temptation to pick up his bowl and drink the rest of the milk, the way he and Matt used to do when they were kids, he carried the bowl to the sink and exchanged it for the coffeepot. He refilled his own cup and topped off Tierney's, then returned to his chair, picked up his coffee and looked across the table at her.

She gazed back at him, which he found both unsettling and refreshing. Most women, he thought, probably wouldn't know what to do with their eyes the morning after a night like that. Not that he had anything to compare this particular morning after with, the night in question being pretty much unparalleled in his experience.

He let out a breath in a long sigh. "Miss Tee, what are we going to do about this?"

She didn't seem to be able to answer, although he saw her throat work and ripple a few times. But she refused to look away, didn't try to avoid his eyes, and for some reason the fact that she wouldn't let herself off the hook touched him.

"Maybe," he said in a gentler tone, "what I should be asking is…what do you *want* to do about this?"

Now she did look away, a guilty ducking of her head and lowering of her lashes to veil her eyes, and a spectacularly unsuccessful attempt to hide a smile behind a quickly raised coffee cup.

He laughed. "Oh, yeah. Me, too."

After a brief but humid silence, Tierney gave her head a determined shake and looked up at him. "I'm sorry, that wasn't fair to you, Wade. I do know what you're asking. We have a professional relationship to consider."

He nodded, watching her closely. "We do. But…something as good as this—and I don't know about you, but for me, that was…as good as it gets. I mean, beyond good. It was—"

She was laughing now, cheeks pink and eyes teary. "Yeah, me, too."

After another of those respectful—awed—silences, Wade shifted in his chair. Shifted gears, serious again. "I guess what I'm asking, is…I think last night happened because you were vulnerable, and maybe I took advantage of that—"

"You didn't."

"Mmm…" The pass, the opportunity to excuse his behavior, was tempting. He shrugged it off, leaned forward, his voice low and tense. "Maybe. But either way, just in case you were thinking that was a one-time thing, I'd hate to think it has to end here just because maybe it shouldn't have happened in the first place. Something this good… damn it, we're good together, Miss Tee. I don't know why, but we are. We can't ignore that."

"No," she whispered.

He saw something in her eyes that made his chest clench. "But?"

She shook her head, worked her throat and looked bravely straight into his eyes again. "But…you have The Job, and I have The Gift. Neither of those things makes for a very optimistic outlook for…whatever this is or might become between us."

"Yeah," he agreed, narrowing his eyes and setting his jaw, determined to be as brave as she was, "I'll grant you, cops do tend to be lousy at relationships."

"And," she went on, "how would you like having to always guard your emotions, twenty-four-seven?"

He smiled crookedly. "Being a cop, I've always pretty much done that anyway."

She acknowledged that with a smile that flickered like a faulty lamp. "Then there's Jeannette. She's only going to get worse, Wade. Harder to deal with. I'll need to keep a constant watch—"

He had no idea what he'd have replied to that. His cell phone, which he'd remembered to put back in its holster when he'd donned his pants, chose that moment to vibrate, startling them both. He unhooked it, glanced at the Caller ID, then punched it on. "Yeah—Callahan."

Tierney watched his face harden as he listened, but she couldn't read him. He was blocking her completely now, and she felt sorry, though not so sure she should be.

It was a short conversation, and on Wade's part, consisted mostly of monosyllables. Then, "On my way," he said, and disconnected. He let out a breath and looked at her.

"Another murder?" she asked softly.

"No. Thank you, God. But we've got a suspect." He pushed back from the table and tilted his head in the general direction of the bathroom. "Mind if I—"

"Of course not. Do you want to shower?"

He was on his feet, now, tucking his phone back in its holster. "I need to go home and get clean clothes, so I'll shower there." He paused to throw her a quick, frowning glance—he was all cop now. "Is there someone you can get to stay with your grandmother?"

She opened her mouth to answer, but he rushed on.

"We've got a warrant to search the suspect's house—last known address, anyway—nobody seems to be there at the moment." He was moving away from her with quick, purposeful strides. She followed him into the living room and stood with her arms wrapped across her waist while he picked up his shirt and shrugged it on. "It'd be helpful if you could be there. Absent any concrete evidence, you might be able to tell if we've got the right guy, at least."

The image of a young police officer's mutilated body flashed across her mind, and with it, like a series of blows inside her head, the terrible fear and pain that had been her final moments. She opened her mouth, but no sound came.

Sympathy, regret, anguish and concern were all there in the way he looked at her. He could keep her from "hearing" his emotions, it seemed, but had forgotten to veil his eyes.

Hold me, Wade. Kiss me and take this fear and pain away.

I know what happened should be a one-time thing. But I don't want to lose what we had last night, either!

Please…just for a moment, hold me. Let me remember…

She gathered the feelings and hurled them at him with all her might, like spears. But of course he hadn't The Gift. He couldn't know.

She drew a shuddering breath. "The girl who helps out in the gallery watches Gran sometimes. Just give me a minute to call her."

Chapter 9

Tierney sat enveloped in silence as Wade drove his unmarked police sedan through Portland's lazy Saturday-morning traffic. The silence was deep and profound, a silence of feelings as well as words.

She knew how much effort it cost him to break it when he finally threw her a glance and muttered, "I'm sorry about this. I really am."

"I know." She said it without thinking, and felt stung when he gave back a bark of sardonic laughter.

"Yeah, I guess you do, don't you."

"Not because of…that. I just…know," she said, studying his rigid profile. "You've gotten very good at blocking me, actually."

He didn't reply. A few minutes later he made several turns, and she recognized the streets, remembered the last time she'd been here. She'd been here with Wade, and then, as now, sitting beside him in his car in a painful silence that felt like the aftermath of a lover's quarrel.

Only then, unlike now, it had been his thoughts—a man's sex thoughts, involuntary, lustful and bawdy—coming through loud and clear that made the silence so awkward. That was then...before he'd gotten so good at blocking.

He looked over at her as if he'd heard *her* thoughts. "What?" he demanded to know as she turned her head quickly to hide them.

She shrugged and replied the only way she could. "Nothing."

Nothing...

There she goes again with that lie. His lips twitched, but he decided to let it go, this time. Because he'd just remembered the last time he'd driven her home with him, and why.

He cleared his throat and in what he hoped was a casual way, said, "Heard anything from my stalker lately?"

She looked at him and then away again. "The *Watcher?*" she pointedly said, correcting him.

She felt irritable, argumentative. And she *wasn't* those things, not normally. Feeling vaguely ashamed but no less angry— *Angry? Is that what I am? Then...why? And at who?*—she said in a tight voice, "No—I haven't."

She felt his quick, questioning glance. Then a shrug. "Guess he found out what he wanted to know and moved on."

But she was remembering that first vivid *impression* from The Watcher, that surge of pure joy. *I found you!*

She'd told Wade about that, but he'd obviously forgotten. Or, she told herself, still teetering on the brink of that inexplicable anger—*Yes, Wade, I'm angry with you, and I'm not sure why!*—he simply insisted on clinging to his own interpretation and was completely ignoring hers.

It seemed so obvious to her, the reason The Watcher—she was sure he was the man they'd met in the Rose Garden, the man with the camera, journalist Cory Pearson—no longer felt the need to shadow Wade. Quite simply, he'd "found" him. She was certain he'd come to the Rose Garden that day intending to speak to him, to make himself—and perhaps his reasons for tracking Wade down—known. And for some reason, he hadn't. *Why?* She hadn't picked up any feelings of fear or anxiety from him when he'd learned Wade was a cop. In fact, she felt sure he'd already known. And yet he'd lost his nerve about coming clean. Again—*why?*

A thought came to her. A notion so incredible, a possibility so emotionally overwhelming, she couldn't keep it inside. She tried her best but must have jerked, winced, made some small sound.

Naturally, Wade's immediate response was a demanding, "What?"

And of course she replied, "Nothing." This wasn't something she could just spring on him out of the blue. And it *was* just a thought…

"Don't lie to me." His voice was harsh with the pain he'd been keeping from her. "Don't shut me out."

When his own words registered with him a moment later, he laughed without feeling the slightest bit amused. "Man, I do hope you got the irony in that."

He paused again, having deduced from her silence that she was hurt, maybe even angry. "Look," he began, then went on in a softer voice, "I've done things with you, felt things... I've never done or felt with any woman before. So...don't shut me out, Miss Tee. Please."

She nodded, made a small throat-sound, then said evenly, "I won't if you won't."

He tightened his jaw, clamped down on his temper. "Damn it, that's not fair."

She exhaled and said tiredly, "No, I guess it isn't."

He felt those candid blue eyes of hers on him but didn't return the look. After a moment she faced forward again, and when she spoke her voice sounded blurred...indistinct. He hoped to God she wasn't crying.

"We didn't get a chance to really talk about this, did we? About what we're going to do."

He pulled into the Hofmeyer's driveway and shifted into Park. He wanted to talk about this, but not now, damn it. He waited a moment, fortifying himself, then turned to her. "How about this? We take it one day...one hour at a time. See what happens."

There was a long pause before she nodded and murmured, "Okay."

For some reason her cooperation didn't make him feel any better. In fact, it almost made him feel worse. And he had no idea why.

It looked to him like gender communications issues didn't get easier just because one of the people involved happened to be psychic.

"I need to shower and shave, put on some clean clothes," he ventured finally. "Shouldn't take long. Do you want to come up and wait? You can nuke some day-old coffee, if you like."

She shook her head. Muttered, "Thanks. I'll just wait here."

Hell. Head movements and words of one syllable seemed to be about it for her right now. He'd gotten more out of suspects in interrogation.

He got out of the car and was about to slam the door when he thought better of it, ducked down to say, "Be right back," then closed it carefully.

Complications, he thought as he stormed up the driveway. *I used to be better at avoiding them. What the hell happened?*

Tierney watched Wade go through the gate between the house and garage, then turn the corner and disappear around the back. It was rapidly becoming too warm in the car, so she opened her door to let some cooler air in. She put her head back against the head rest and closed her eyes, feeling bruised in mind and spirit, buffeted by storms of emotion— her own, for a change. How had she let this happen?

She knew better, too. People like her weren't cut out for entanglements like this. The emotional strain was simply too much. Especially now. On top of everything she had to deal with.

Lonely!

The emotional cannonball seemed to come out of nowhere. And no one. Tierney jerked upright and looked around, but there wasn't a soul in sight, not on the street, or in any of the yards. In fact, the only living creature abroad in the neighborhood appeared to be a very fat, very bored-looking basset hound sitting in the middle of the flagstone path that led to the gate through which Wade had just passed.

Lonely!

"No," Tierney whispered, staring at the animal, "don't tell me."

The basset gazed at her with a superior expression of the type usually associated with British butlers.

She got out of the car and squatted down so as to be more on a level with the creature. "Okay, dog," she muttered. "What'sa matter, hmm? Are you the one who's lonely?"

Lonely...curious...hopeful...

The hound heaved his massive hind end off the pavers and waddled toward her without haste, nose to the ground, ears dragging. Tierney met him halfway, lowered herself into a half crouch and held out her hand for the animal to sniff. She wasn't terribly experienced with dogs, but it seemed to her this was what people did when meeting a strange one.

This dog, however, displayed no interest whatsoever in her offering. He turned his head and gazed dolefully down the street.

Since he didn't appear to possess the energy required to actually bite anyone, Tierney decided to take the risk of patting him on the head.

Love! Adoration!

Amazing, Tierney thought, collapsing onto her knees beside the dog and silently laughing. *Who would have guessed?*

Adoration! Devotion!

Tears stung her eyes. The dog continued to regard her with what seemed to be utter disdain as she fondled his long silky ears and murmured dopey endearments.

"Unbelievable," Wade said.

Tierney looked up and her heart performed an impossible maneuver.

He was freshly shaven and showered, dressed in tan slacks and a light blue shirt open, as always, at the neck. A navy-blue blazer was slung over one shoulder, hanging from a crooked finger. His eyes were so vivid a blue it made her own eyes smart to look into them.

"This is the sweetest dog," she said, hiding her shakiness with laughter. "Is he yours?"

"Sweet. You're kidding, right?" He snorted. "The mutt smells like a rancid landfill. On a hot day."

"Oh, he does not." She looked down at the dog, who had turned his head to stare haughtily at Wade over one shoulder. "What's his name?"

"Bruno. And if he hasn't gassed you out yet, give him a minute. He prefers sneak attacks. He's my landlords' dog, and the bane of my existence. I would have caught me a stalker the other night if it hadn't been for this lazy—"

"He's got a nervous stomach," Tierney informed him as she got to her feet, brushing off her jeans. She gave Wade an accusing look. "*You* make him nervous, actually. He knows you don't like him."

"Unbelievable," he breathed, gazing at her in wonderment. "I leave you alone for ten minutes and you become a dog whisperer."

He'd done some whispering with himself during those ten minutes, a good part of which had been spent staring at his own countenance in the mirror. What he'd seen there hadn't made him happy. He was used to thinking of himself as one of the good guys, and didn't much care for the complete and total jackass looking back at him.

The first thing he'd reminded himself was that, whatever was going on with Tierney, it wasn't in any way, shape or form her fault. As far as the job and the case went, she was doing what she'd been called on to do. Doing it even though it was causing her a considerable amount of pain and suffering, and even though she had enough on her plate already just trying to look after a grandmother with Alzheimer's. And as for what happened between them last night…well, no matter what *she* said, he knew that was on him.

The second thing? Completely aside from what had happened between them last night, she was first and foremost his partner. She should be able to trust him to look out for her. And she definitely deserved better than she'd gotten from him so far.

Well—not counting the sex. He didn't see how he was ever going to top last night in that department. Assuming he ever got a chance to try.

Yeah, he told himself, gazing down into her radiant face and shimmering eyes, *this is the way to go. Partners. Keep things on a strictly professional basis between us. Until we get this other thing figured out, anyway…*

At least it looked like she'd gotten over being mad at him, or whatever it was that had been bothering her.

"You want me to take you to pick up your car before we head out to the suspect's place?" he asked as he fished his keys out of his pocket.

Her eyes followed Bruno as he went ambling off toward his favorite shady spot under the rhododendrons. Then she gave Wade a distracted smile that faded as he watched, and murmured, "I'd rather go with you—if that's okay."

She's dreading this, he thought. And then, in mild surprise, *Man, I'm getting pretty good at this empathy thing.*

He reached out one arm, hooked it around her neck and drew her close, allowing himself one brief moment, no more. *Partners...*

He closed his eyes, exhaled, then kissed the top of her head and let her go. When he did, something kicked him painfully under his ribs.

Partners? Who am I kidding?

"Mind if I ask who this person is—and how you found him?" Tierney asked.

"Traffic tickets." Wade smiled darkly, aware that at the moment they were speeding through considerably more traffic than there'd been earlier this morning and he was in some danger of receiving a citation himself. He didn't want to use his stick-on lights and siren on the way to meet SWAT on the off chance their suspect was in the vicinity, after all.

"Traffic tickets?" He felt her eyes on him as she waited for his explanation.

He glanced in his mirrors and executed an illegal lane change before giving her one.

"Yeah...since Officer Williams was a traffic cop, we figured maybe this creep targeted her because she'd given him one recently. Came up with a whole slew of possibles based on age and gender, then searched those for backgrounds that fit the profile you gave us. That knocked the list all the way down to seven. Interviews made it three— a small enough number that we were able to get warrants to search phone and credit card records. That's where we hit paydirt. Phone records were a bust, but turns out one of our candidates—fellow by the name of James Jeffry Larson, known in his checkered past as J.J.—had some expense items that dovetailed nicely with several of the murders." He paused for a tire squeal and leaned into a high-speed turn. When the car had stopped fishtailing, he smiled grimly at the mirrors and then at the street ahead. "Now I guess we'll see if those were just coincidences, or if this is our guy."

There was no immediate response from his passenger, but he could tell she was looking at him. He risked a glance and found something in those blue eyes of hers that made a jolt of purely masculine elation go shooting through him—probably an unnecessary boost to the adrenaline already there.

"What?" he said, and braced for her usual evasive reply.

It didn't come. "It's pretty amazing, what you do," she said as she shifted her gaze to the front again. "The police work, I mean. In fact, I really don't know why you needed me."

He gave her another quick look, wondering if she was regretting the circumstances that had brought them together. Maybe wishing they hadn't happened?

"Just basic detective work, Miss Tee. A whole lot of man-hours, most of them not mine, by the way. The kind of eye-crossingly boring stuff you don't get to see on those TV cop shows. And yeah, we probably would have gotten here eventually without you. But not before who knows how many other women had to die unspeakable deaths. Die in terror and pain." He pulled his car into the parking area where the SWAT van and other members of his team had gathered, waiting for him. He cut the motor, pulled the keys and turned in the seat to face her.

"You shut him down, Tierney," he said quietly. "I know it cost you. But those women the slime bag *didn't* get to kill? That's on you."

He watched her eyes fill and knew he didn't dare touch her. He felt a weakening in his muscles and a cold knot in the pit of his stomach. Pure fear. What was the woman doing to him?

She looked away from him…he saw her swallow, and blink her vision clear as she stared through the windshield. Then she went sheet-white.

"Wade—this is—"

"The park where the next-to-last victim was found. Your first. Yeah," he said with a grim smile, "that's one of those little things that might be coincidence—or not. The guy, J. J. Larson, lives just five blocks from here."

He told her to stay put, then got out of the car and went to confer with the other members of the task force.

Ed Francks came to meet him, stopped him a short distance from the rest of the take-down team and handed him a vest. "Hey, partner, where's your cryst—"

Wade cut him off right there. "Don't say it, Ed. Not you, too. I swear to God—" He gave it up, exhaled and pointed with a head jerk. "She's with me. In the car."

"Got one of these for her, too. Want me to—"

"I'll take it."

He looked up from what he was doing, strapping on the vest, getting his weapon and badge squared away. "What're you laughin' at?"

"Me? I ain't laughin'. Who's laughing?"

"Grinnin' like a fool, then."

"That right? Well, since you mention fools, I'm remembering some things *you* said last time we were together in this park. Something about…what was it? Oh yeah… cheerleaders…"

Wade squinted his eyes in a mock grimace of pain. "Ed, you and me go back a long way. Doesn't mean I won't kick your ass."

That got him a hoot of friendly derision. Then a semi-serious, "Just watchin' out for you, man." Then a genuinely serious, "You just watch out for that little lady."

"Yeah." Wade gave his vest a final hitch and took the smaller one Francks handed him. "See you there, man."

The two men touched knuckles…grasped thumbs. Which was as close to embracing as most cops get.

The take-down team rolled silently onto the suspect's street from opposite ends, leaving vehicles parked in strategic positions in order to block it. If the suspect was on the premises and took a notion to flee, he'd have to do it on foot.

Wade pulled his unmarked gray sedan in behind the SWAT van where it would be screened from the suspect's house and any flying bullets—or emotions—in case things went bad. He shut it down and pocketed the keys.

"Wait here until I come for you," he said tersely. "I mean it, Miss Tee. Stay put and keep your head down."

"I will." It was a whisper. Her lips looked pinched, her cheeks pale. He couldn't bring himself to look at her eyes.

Lord, how he wanted to kiss her.

She nodded and managed a smile, and he knew he'd forgotten to block. And for once, didn't give a damn. He opened the door, got out, hit the safety locks and slammed the door. And walked quickly off to join his team.

Things went off like clockwork.

Communicating with hand signals, the team members took up their positions, surrounding the house and blocking every possible exit. When he was satisfied everyone was in place, Wade rapped on the front door with his knuckles—taking care to stand to one side in case the suspect should take a notion to open fire—and yelled out the customary command.

"James Larson, this is Portland P.D. We have a warrant to search the premises. Open up, please."

After a brief wait, another knock, with his fist this time. "Police, Mr. Larson. Open the door."

Wait a short three-count. Try the doorknob. *Locked.* A nod to the SWAT guys standing by with the ram. A huge surge of adrenaline as the door crashed open, and officers in helmets and body armor with weapons at full ready made their way through the rooms, one by one, leapfrogging, taking turns covering each other.

"Clear!"

Shift…point. "Clear!"

Satisfied finally that the perp was not on the premises, everyone stood down, still jumped up on the adrenaline they didn't get to use and now didn't quite know what to do with. They looked around, looked at each other, took deep breaths, relaxed their arms, stowed their weapons. But nobody smiled. Not yet.

Wade was on his way down the front steps, going to get Tierney, when one of the task force detectives, Ochoa, stuck his head out the door and gestured for him to come back. "Callahan, you better see this." The edge of suppressed excitement in Detective Ochoa's voice was impossible to miss.

Wade followed him through completely unremarkable rooms, filled with the sort of shabby, unremarkable stuff he'd seen a thousand times before, in homes of perps and victims alike. Nothing to tell him whether James Jeffry Larson was capable of stalking, kidnapping, systematically and gruesomely torturing and murdering seven innocent women.

Until he stepped into the garage.

Like a lot of suburban garages, this one had been finished inside for living space rather than housing cars, probably without city permits being involved, since it still looked like a normal garage from the outside. Part of this garage contained the kind of stuff you'd expect in an add-on room—laundry facilities, pool table, treadmill, small bar with an extra fridge. Except for the washer and dryer, none of these things appeared to have been used in a while. Most likely installed by a former resident, Wade thought.

Ochoa led him through the clutter to a small room that had been partitioned off on the far side of the two-car garage. The door to the room stood open, and Wade could see a couple more of his detectives moving around inside.

"Santa's been good to us this year," Ochoa said gleefully, seemingly unaware they were a long way from Christmas.

Wade glanced at Ochoa's grim but triumphant face and stepped through the door. And realized it wasn't going to be necessary for Tierney to come in, after all.

It was all there. What every homicide cop dreams of finding in a suspect's house. The trophies, photos, articles clipped from newspapers and magazines covering every murder, every victim. Photos taken of his victims while

they were alive and happy, and later when they very much
were not, tacked up on every wall like a gruesome parody
of an art gallery.

Art gallery…

"Have a look." Ed Francks' voice was a low rumble only
Wade could have recognized as fury.

Wade took the piece of newsprint Ed handed him and
felt his soul freeze and his body go numb. Staring up at him
in newspaper headline black and white were the words:
Does PPD Have A Crystal Ball?

They were all over the desktop, tacked to a corkboard
on the wall beside it. Newspaper articles about the Portland
cop with the crystal ball. Grainy photos of Tierney, circled
in red marker, slashed, mutilated.

It was his worst fear made real.

A wave of nausea hit him. He felt cold, light-headed.
Through the ringing in his ears he heard someone ask him
if he was okay. He didn't have any idea what he answered.

The next thing he knew he was outside that house and
running down the street. Running as fast as he ever had in
his life, he rounded the SWAT van. And now he could see
Tierney's face through his car's windshield. She had both
hands up, covering the bottom half of her face, and above
them her eyes were wide with horror.

My God, what am I doing?

He jolted to a halt, heart pounding, knees shaking, and put
out a hand, a gesture meant to reassure her and at the same
time stop himself. Stop the terrible avalanche of emotions
he knew she must be feeling like a physical assault.

He managed to get the door unlocked and jerked it open.

"Tee, I'm sorry. I'm sorry…" He flung himself into the

driver's seat and stared up at the headliner, breathing hard. "God…I'm so sorry."

"Wade…" Her voice sounded small and scared, like a child trying not to cry.

He shook his head. He'd never wanted so much to touch someone. Reach out for her, wrap her up in his arms and hold her. He would, too, but not here. Not now. First he had to get her away from this place. As far away and as fast as he possibly could.

He thought about what would have happened to her if he'd taken her into that house. Thought about what she'd have had to experience. The horrors.

Bile rose into his throat. He stabbed the keys blindly at the ignition a couple of times before it occurred to him he might not be in fit condition to drive anywhere at the moment, and he gave up and pounded impotently on the steering wheel with a clenched fist instead.

"Sorry," he muttered again. It seemed all he was capable of saying to her.

Someone rapped sharply on the car window, inches from his elbow. He looked up to find Ed Francks' dark face and worried eyes peering in at him. He ran the window down and Ed's fingers curved over the edge and followed it the last half of the way.

"Hey, man, you okay?" He didn't wait for Wade's reply, but moved the look of concern and compassion past him to where Tierney sat silent and pale.

"Yeah," Wade growled, and it was so obvious a lie he amended it to, "will be."

"She needs to be away from here. You want me to drive her—"

"No. Stay here. Make sure they get every scrap of evidence, every hair, fiber and print. I want this guy, Ed. I want him caught. Locked up."

Which was another lie. He wanted him *dead*. And he knew his old partner understood when he gave the window-sill a slap and stood back, his jaw set and eyes like obsidian.

"We'll take care of things here," Ed said quietly. "You go on—get *her* to a safe place. And keep her there until we get the sonofabitch, okay?"

"Count on it." Wade made another try with the keys and this time his hand was steady as a rock.

Chapter 10

Once again Wade drove with the window down, one-handed, elbow on the sill and his hand across the lower part of his face. For once, though, Tierney didn't mind that he was walling himself off from her in every way he could.

Although she didn't blame him for it, she was still shaky from that terrible blast of emotion he'd hit her with. It had been the worst thing she'd ever experienced, all the horror of the crime scenes and the killer's twisted mind amplified a thousand times by Wade's own rage and fear.

Fear of what might happen...to me.

It wasn't until she realized they were heading in the wrong direction for downtown that she summoned the will and courage to attempt to penetrate that wall. It took her one abortive try and a throat-clearing before she was able to ask, "Are you taking me to pick up my car?"

He moved his hand, cleared gravel from his own throat. He glanced at her, then back forward, and after a long pause, shook his head. "No. Your car stays where it is until impound can get it under lock and key. In the meantime, I'm going to be driving you wherever you need to go. As of about fifteen minutes ago, you are under twenty-four-hour police protection. I, or someone on the task force, is going to be with you 'round the clock. Understand?" He threw her another look, this one as hard and grim as any she'd ever seen from him. "No arguments."

"I wasn't going to give you any," Tierney said quietly. "But I do think I deserve to know why. I know you found something in that house. Something terrible. Something you don't want to tell me about." She laughed shakily. "Trust me, Wade, nothing you tell me could possibly be worse than what I've been imagining."

The side of his face she could see formed an ironic smile. "I keep forgetting you don't read minds." There was another long pause, then an exhalation.

"Okay, for starters, he's definitely our guy. And he's in the wind. He's been derailed, thwarted, and for that…he blames you. He's read those damn newspaper articles about the department consulting 'our crystal ball,' and is scared enough by the notion of a psychic on his trail that he's gone to ground. For now. But he won't stay there."

They'd stopped at a traffic light. He scrubbed a hand over his face, then turned to look at her. His eyes were red-rimmed but brilliant and hard as diamonds. "He's targeted you as his next victim. He's got pictures of you. Tacked up all over the place. And he's done…to those pictures…what he means—ah, *hell*."

The light changed. The car moved forward, and Tierney watched trees and cars and buildings go by in a shimmering blur. The palms of her hands and the soles of her feet felt tingly. She swallowed. "Does he know where I live?"

This time the glance he gave her was bleak. "I don't know, Miss Tee."

But she felt his fear. "You think he might, though, don't you?" And she fought to keep her own desperate terror out of her voice. *Oh God...Jennie. Gran...dearest Gran. How I wish I could hear you!*

"Or that he can at least find out." Wade whipped the car into a no-parking zone near the front of the gallery and cut the engine. He gave her a stay-put gesture, then got out and surveyed the street and sidewalks in every direction as he circled briskly around to her side of the vehicle. He opened her door and held out a hand.

"I don't think he's here," Tierney said breathlessly as she gave him hers. "I can't feel him, anyway."

"Thank God for that." Taking her elbow in a firm grip, he hurried her into the gallery and flipped over the Closed sign on the front door.

"Hi, welcome to Jeanette's Gallery, my name is Clair, just let me know if there's anything I can help you with..." Clair Yee, the Reed College freshman who helped out with the gallery and Jeannètte-sitting when Tierney had to be away for more than an hour at a time, came in through the back door, giving off waves of worry and concern—and a little bit of annoyance she was trying to suppress.

She halted in her tracks when she saw Tierney and

Wade, and said, "Oh! Oh, my God," in the overly dramatic fashion of the young. "I am *so* glad you're back."

Tierney's heart rate kicked into high. "What's wrong? Is Gran—"

"I didn't know what to do. I mean, I *know* she gets upset sometimes, and it's not like I don't *know*... I mean, I've dealt with her before, I'm sort of used to her moods..."

Wade gave Tierney's elbow a little squeeze, then released it and fell back to let her climb the stairs side-by-side with Clair.

"I mean, she just got so *upset.* Just all of a sudden, and for no reason, you know? One minute she's sitting there at the table working on this really pretty Monet jigsaw puzzle I got for her, and then all of a sudden she just, like, gets up and starts crying, and walking back and forth, back and forth. I didn't know what to do. I mean, should I have called 9-1-1?"

"It's all right," Tierney said soothingly. "It's hard to know what might have gotten into her. Maybe she had a memory, or—" She broke off as a familiar little pain stabbed at her heart. "Clair, how long ago did this happen?"

"Oh, gosh. I'm not sure...not that long. Half an hour...forty-five minutes, maybe? I haven't let her out of my sight since, though, I swear—I mean, until I heard the dinger just now. I hope—"

"No, no— Clair, it's all right. Really. I'm sure she'll be fine. She'll settle down, now that I'm..." She stood on the landing and grasped for a breath. The shivery thrill of emotion inside her was moving dangerously close to tears. She glanced over her shoulder to see what had become of Wade, but judging from the thumps and bangs resonating from the rooms below, he was still checking doors and dead bolt locks. "You know," she said to Clair, "I think I'm going to close up early today, anyway, so why don't you just go ahead and go home now? Make sure you leave me your hours, though, okay?"

"Oh." The girl's expression was doubtful but her emotions exuded relief and joy. "Well...if you're sure..."

"I'm sure—and, Clair, you're a dear to come at short notice like this. Thanks."

"Oh, no problem, Tee. Any time." She went skipping down the stairs like a dog that had just been let off her leash.

Tierney drew in a breath that hurt her chest, then unlocked the door and pushed it open.

Jeannette was sitting on the couch, staring straight ahead and rocking...rocking. Her hands were clasped together in her lap and her face was streaked with tears.

"Jennie, darling," Tierney called softly as she moved forward on uncertain legs, "it's me...Tee."

Her grandmother's grief-stricken face swiveled toward her, coming slowly alight now, with hope. "Tee?" Her voice sounded quavery and frail, an old, old woman's voice. "Is it you? I thought..."

"I know...I know." Tierney sank onto the couch and gathered her grandmother into her arms, crooning to her like a mother to a frightened child. "It's all right, Jennie, dear...it's all right. I'm here now. Tee's here." As she crooned the words of comfort she let the tears come, and they were tears of joy mixed with inexpressible sorrow.

Oh, Gran, you heard me, didn't you? You heard me, just the way you used to. You are *still here, aren't you? Gran...can you hear me now? Do you know I love you?*

And she heard the reply, faint but unmistakable. *My dearest child. I love you, too.*

Wade's inspection of the gallery's security situation left him with two conclusions. One, a determined serial killer could get into the place easily, no problem. Like a hot knife through butter. And two, no way in hell could he allow his "crystal ball" to stay here.

His first impulse was to march up the stairs and tell her so, but something of her "gift" must have rubbed off on him, because he was able to stop himself before he did something stupid. Because he knew exactly what her reaction to *that* would be—no doubt whatsoever.

So, since he already knew moving Tierney and her grandmother to a safe house was going to be out of the question, for now he was going to have to make do with assigning a couple of uniforms to look out for them. During the day, anyway. Nights…well, he figured he could handle those himself.

Figuring he'd get less argument if it was already a done deal, he called Nola with his request and got the first protection detail assigned and on their way before he headed upstairs to break the news to Tierney.

On the landing at the top of the stairs he paused, frowning. *Door standing open, unlocked. Not good.* He'd have to remind Tierney to be more careful. Just because *he* happened to be somewhere on the premises didn't mean she could let her guard down. Not even for a minute. Not until this sicko was caught. *Or dead.*

He shut the door carefully behind him, set the dead bolt and walked into the living room. And every thought of lectures and scolding melted away into nothing, leaving him with nothing but an aching knot smack in the middle of his chest.

He walked over and lowered himself into the easy chair placed at a right angle to the couch where Tierney sat holding and rocking her grandmother, patting the old lady's back. As if, he thought, Tierney was the parent and Jeannette a distraught teenager with a broken heart.

He was rubbing absently at the knot in his chest when Tierney looked up and smiled radiantly at him.

"She heard me, Wade," she said, laughing through her tears. "Just like she used to. We had this connection—she always knew when I was in trouble, or upset…hurt. It's still there. It isn't gone, not completely. Oh, Wade…" She closed her eyes tightly and her face seemed to crumple.

Wade leaned back in the chair, stretched out his legs and stared up at the ceiling. Let out a breath, long and slow.

When had it happened? When had these two women gotten so far under his skin that even he knew there was no way in hell he'd ever get them out?

It began to dawn on him then, that the ache in his chest was longing. And that what he was longing for was something he didn't even know he'd been missing. It was all tangled up with memories, the ones he had and the ones he didn't. Family…the mom and dad who'd raised him, loved him—he loved them, too, of course, and remembered to phone them now and then. The mother and father he couldn't remember except in nightmares. The brother he'd somehow lost touch with. His only brother…Matt.

It was the angel, Wade.

He's a boy angel. Like us, only bigger.

He felt restless suddenly. Itchy—the way he did when a case wasn't coming along well. When the evidence wasn't making sense…clues not adding up.

He stood up, and Tierney's misty gaze followed him. He touched her hair gently…resisted the desire to let his fingers linger in its softness. "Your protection's on its way. I'll be downstairs—they'll need to be let in and briefed."

"You're going." It wasn't a question.

"Got to get back to work. There's going to be a ton of evidence to go through once the techs get done with that house. I'll be back, though—might be late, so don't wait up. Just leave me a pillow and a blanket and I'll make myself comfortable on the couch."

She nodded, a little smile flirting with the corners of her mouth. His stomach gave a playful flip, and he thought again of the things he'd been missing. He rested his hand on her head for a moment, but it wasn't nearly enough, so he leaned down and kissed her forehead.

And that wasn't enough, either. Not nearly.

Later that evening, several time zones away on a small lake somewhere in South Carolina, Samantha Pearson sat cross-legged on a floating dock and watched the fireflies wink and dance in the darkening woods. The night lay thick and warm around her. There'd been a thunderstorm earlier, but its brief respite from the heat and humidity was only a memory.

Somewhere a whip-poor-will was singing his little heart out; the frog chorus was working up to a frenzy, and from across the lake came the intermittent scream of a locust. And all in the hope of snagging a mate, Sam thought resentfully. *The whole damn world is teeming with critters bent on hooking up, and here I am, a married woman, alone. Where's the justice in that?*

The dock creaked suddenly, but before she could turn around, a pair of warm hands came from behind to cover her eyes. She gasped, and her heart lurched and began to pound, almost in sync with the whip-poor-will's frantic song.

"Cory!" She twisted in his arms and hurled herself against his chest, toppling him onto his back. The dock bobbed giddily, like a cork on a choppy sea.

"Whoa, woman, don't you even look before you throw yourself at a man? What if I was an ax-murderer or a deranged—"

"Don't you think I know my own husband's hands? Hush up and kiss me, Pearse. I've been 'bout to die of loneliness."

"Loneliness? Oh, is that what we're calling it? I can think of another word. Starts with 'H', rhymes with corn— umphf…" It was a good bit later before he was able to complete the thought, in a considerably weaker and breathier voice. "Sammie June…sweetheart… I've only been gone four days."

"Well, I know that, but it seems like years."

After that, there wasn't much talking. The dock rocked gently under the stars.

It was nearly midnight when Wade left police headquarters in downtown Portland. He made a detour to his place to pick up a change of clothes and his shaving stuff, and another to an all-night supermarket and finally pulled up in front of Jeannette's Gallery at a little after one in the morning. He sent the two unis on guard duty home with his thanks and a backslap, and carried his overnighter and a brace of plastic grocery bags up the stairs to Tierney's apartment.

He let himself in with the keys she'd given him, then, quietly as he could, set the overnighter and groceries down and locked up behind him. A light had been left on in the kitchen—enough to see by. The TV was on, muted, tuned to an all-night high-stakes poker game, and in its glow he could see Tierney lying on the couch, sound asleep.

He felt an uneven jerking sensation inside his chest, as if a very small puppy was playing tug-of-war with his heart.

Leaving his overnighter where it was, he carried the grocery bags into the kitchen and unloaded beer, ground beef and a few other odd essentials into the refrigerator. Toaster waffles went in the freezer, burger buns and coffee on the countertop. When he went back to the living room he found Tierney awake, sitting up, and in the middle of a huge yawn.

"You weren't supposed to wait up for me," he said, trying to sound scolding.

She gulped the yawn down and murmured, "I was sleeping. That's not waiting up. That's…" She yawned again.

"Mmm, hmm…right." Seeing no reason at all why he shouldn't, he leaned over the back of the couch and kissed her neck. Her skin was moist and warm, and smelled of soap and cool green gardens. Caught again in midyawn, she gave him a startled look, and one hand rose to touch his hair as if it had decided to do so all on its own.

"Quit yawning, Doyle," he whispered, "so I can kiss you properly."

She sighed without sound, a subtle relaxing of head and neck that brought her mouth into perfect alignment with his. He cradled her head between his hands and stroked the soft delicate underside of her jaw with his fingertips as he let his lips caress…his tongue savor…his teeth delicately measure…and his mind soak in all the shapes and textures and flavors of that mouth. Then he threw patient exploration to the winds and plunged into its depths and lost himself there, heart and soul.

At some point, having relinquished support of her head to the couch cushions, his hands discovered what his eyes had seen and his mind not registered. She was wearing a loose-fitting nightgown made of something soft, with thin shoulder straps made of some kind of ribbon, and plenty of room at the low neckline for his hands to slip inside.

Her skin was warm and sleek, like the pelt of some magnificent animal…a panther or leopard. Her breasts filled his hands as if made for that purpose and no other, and the nipples formed delicate buds between his thumbs and forefingers.

She arched her back, pushed her breasts into his hands…then broke from him suddenly, shockingly. Ripping her mouth away from his, she sat up straight, trembling. "I thought…we hadn't decided…what to do about this."

"One day at a time," Wade growled, resting his elbows on the back of the couch and rocking slightly…easing himself. "One minute. And at this minute—" Realizing he didn't need to say it, he stopped and simply looked at her.

She looked back at him and said nothing.

He smiled. "I may not have your gift, darlin', but I know you feel the same way I do. It's why you waited up for me, isn't it? You could have left me a pillow and a blanket, like

I told you." He waited, and when she still didn't say anything, added a gentle, "Why didn't you?"

"I wanted…" She stopped, licked her lips.

"Yeah," he said softly, "me, too."

He rounded the end of the couch and she stood up to meet him. His plan had been to scoop her up in some grand passionate gesture and carry her off to her bedroom, but something in her face…in her eyes…stopped him. He halted, facing her, and reached for her hands. Entwined his fingers with hers.

"Tee, don't make this more complicated than it is." He said it in a breaking voice, something he hadn't expected. His face felt rigid, as though the muscles there were fighting for control over the emotions that had somehow taken over his being. "It's just two people…you and me…making love."

She gazed at him for a long moment. Then, as quickly, as shockingly as she'd broken from him, she reached up, took his face between her hands, stood on tiptoe and kissed him. Kissed him deeply, fervently, in a way that left no more doubts, no more questions.

Except for one, maybe. It flashed through Wade's mind to wonder what it was she'd read in him when she'd looked at him for that time…that seemingly endless moment. But then again, he was pretty sure he already knew.

He did sweep her up into his arms, then, and she wrapped her arms around his neck and gave a soft giggle of pleasure.

"That bed of yours…you mentioned it's big?"

She nodded, bumping her forehead against his, and breathlessly whispered, "And comfortable. Um…in case you were wondering, it's thataway."

"I have condoms," he said in a gruff murmur as he carried her into her bedroom. "I stopped at the store."

She laughed softly. "Callahan, I think that train has left the station."

It was different that night—the sex. Different, though no less overwhelming. Tierney couldn't have said for sure why, except that it may have had something to do with the words Wade had used to describe it.

Two people…making love…

That, and what she'd *felt* from him, just before she'd kissed him.

At first, though, in her bedroom, alone with him, she felt nervous…shaky. Shy, as if she'd never made love with this man—maybe *any* man—before.

While he sat on the foot of the bed and took off his shoes, she folded back the covers…plumped the pillows…little wifely gestures that felt strange to her. Then she stood self-consciously and watched him as he rose and unbuckled his belt.

Somber-faced, he watched her eyes watching him as he tugged his shirt from the waistband of his pants, unbuttoned the cuffs, first, then the front.

She stepped closer, reached out and pushed the two halves of his shirt apart, then slowly over his shoulders. Still clinging to his gaze, she hooked a thumb under one strap of her nightgown and drew it over her shoulder. She was about to do the same to the other when his hand covered hers, stopping her, and his feelings flowed over her like a crystal cascade, like the little waterfalls that bathed the southern slope of the Columbia River Gorge, nurturing moss and ferns and delicate flowers. She nodded, biting her lip as shivers of anticipation rippled through her and her nipples budded against the caressing fabric of her gown.

Wade smiled as he watched the sculpt of her breasts rise in bold relief under her nightgown, and blessed the light from the streetlamps outside her bedroom windows that made it possible. If he'd had his way he'd have all the lights blazing, the better to drink in the sight of her body. He wanted to see her, every detail, every freckle. He wanted to witness the changes heat and passion brought to her eyes…her skin.

But he wouldn't ask that of her, not tonight. Someday soon he would, but she was nervous tonight. And for some reason that only made her more precious to him. He'd never felt such tenderness before. Not for any woman.

Not for anyone.

Quickly, then, he hauled his undershirt up his back and over his head and pitched it in roughly the same direction he'd just tossed his shirt. And he caught his breath when Tierney's hand came to rest on his chest.

His muscles felt cramped with thwarted urges…to reach for her, pull her against him, hold her tightly, push into her…all the things his male imperative demanded he do, sooner rather than later. But he wouldn't allow them, not yet. He sucked in a breath and held himself still and let her fingers wander where they wished…and then her mouth and her teeth and tongue.

Light-headed for lack of breath, he finally exhaled and murmured, "Tee…please." She lifted brilliant eyes to his, and he laughed painfully. "To quote someone I heard recently…I'd like very much to see you naked."

She smiled, biting down on her lower lip, and he put his hands on her shoulders and eased the straps of her night-gown over her shoulders…down her arms. She drew her arms free, and the gown fluttered to the floor.

She stood trembling, naked under his eager gaze, making no move to cover herself even though her every instinct longed to do so. *Because I want to give him this…me. I do.*

But I wonder if he knows how vulnerable I feel.

A moment later she knew he did.

He drew a shaken-sounding breath and wrapped her in his arms, cupped her head in his hand, tucked her face in the hollow of his neck and buried his face in her hair. And simply held her.

She no longer felt vulnerable, not even a little bit. She felt invincible, as if the strongest armor in the world sur-rounded her. She felt protected and powerful, but gentle, too, because she could afford to be. She felt confident she could move mountains…and was utterly secure in knowing she didn't have to.

I wonder…can you tell me, Wade? Is this what it feels like to be loved?

It was different tonight—the lovemaking. Wade couldn't remember ever having felt like this before. None of the usual masculine issues—and he suspected they were pretty much universal among males—seemed to matter to him.

There were no doubts or insecurities, no thoughts about whether he was the best lover she'd ever known, or even simply a good one. He didn't think, *Is this touch going to pleasure her? Has any man ever touched her this way?* He felt nothing of ego, had no conscious wish to make her go wild with desire for the sake of his own pride…none of those selfish little thoughts that lurked in the back of most men's minds when they made love to a woman. In fact, he couldn't recall thinking at all.

Afterward he couldn't even recall what they'd done, precisely. He remembered a perfect melding of his body with hers, without any words being spoken. Remembered losing track of where he left off and she began, and feelings so intense there wasn't anything to be done but surrender himself to them and let them carry him where they would.

He remembered a climax that came for them both at the same moment, as naturally and effortlessly as the sun rising.

And thinking, just before sleep came for him, *I wonder…can you tell me, Miss Tee? Is this what it feels like to make* love?

He woke in darkness. Suffocating, absolute darkness.

His heart raced, pounded. He was sweating and shaking, and he wanted desperately to cry. The sobs were like something alive inside his chest, hurting him, fighting to get out.

But he was too big to cry. *Don't want to be a baby. I'm not a baby! I'm not!*

So he didn't cry.

Then came the noise. Terrible noises—deafening. Things crashing, breaking, thumps and bangs, voices yelling…screaming. He wanted to put his hands over his ears to shut out the sounds of screaming…yelling. But for some reason he couldn't.

"Mama! Mama!"

Somebody was saying that, sobbing—not him. *It's not me, it's not me! I'm too big to cry for my mama!*

But someone was. He could hear them clearly, small frightened voices whimpering, "Mommy…"

And then, finally…like a warm blanket on a cold, cold night…like a soft sweet breeze carrying promises of summer…he heard the *other* voice, the one he'd been waiting for, praying for. The one he'd known all along would come and save him.

Shh… It's okay…it's gonna be okay. It's over. You're safe now. It's okay…

He felt safe, then. And he hunkered down in the warm darkness and waited for the crashing and banging and screaming and yelling to stop and the lights to turn on. Lights so bright they hurt his eyes. So bright…

He opened his eyes, but the only light was the pale wash from streetlights outside uncurtained windows.

There were arms around him, strong and gentle…a damp cheek pressed against his…a scent that reminded him of rain-fresh gardens. And a voice, one he knew, whispered the familiar words from his dream…

"Shh…it's okay, it's okay, my love. You're safe now. I'm here. Tee's here…"

Chapter 11

The next time Wade woke it was to find sunlight pouring into the room through those same uncurtained windows, and Tierney raised up on one elbow with her head propped on her hand, gazing somberly down at him.

Memories of the night before came swiftly. In a voice gruff with morning and emotion, he growled, "What?"

She hesitated while a smile came and went briefly, then answered him. "Just looking at you."

"And?"

"Seeing you here…like this…makes me happy."

He lifted one hand and traced the line of her jaw with a fingertip. "And yet, this is not a happy face. How come?"

He saw a swallow ripple her throat before she rolled away from him and sat up, clutching a rumpled sheet around herself.

"Miss Tee?"

She didn't answer.

In the silence he heard bells ringing somewhere in the distance and remembered it was Sunday. *Sunday morning...* And he thought of a song from a long time ago, something his parents had listened to, probably. He couldn't really recall the words to it, mostly just the way it had made him feel. Lonely...wishing again for that something he couldn't quite remember. *Sunday mornin', comin' down...*

"Tierney," he began again, and she threw the reply at him over her shoulder as she stood up, breathless, almost angry. "Because I can't let myself get too used to it."

"Wha— Wait a minute." He hitched himself up, lunged and caught her hand. Held it fast against her resistance. "Okay, I'm confused here. What's wrong with getting used to me being in your bed?"

She stared at him for a long time, then relented and allowed him to reel her in. She sat slumped on the side of the bed and he took her face in his hand and turned it gently toward him. "Why not, Tee?" The stark misery in her eyes made him feel both achy and in some deep part of him, scared. "We're good together. In fact, we just seem to get better and better. What's wrong with making this a habit?"

She closed her eyes and turned her face away from his hand, though not before he saw the glitter of moisture through her lashes. She drew a weary-sounding breath. "I thought we already had this conversation."

"Sure we did." Then, because he figured his arguments might carry more weight with her if he wasn't bare naked when he presented them, he drew his knees up and draped some covers over them. Then his arms. "As I recall, the objections to us having a relationship had to do with my job, your 'gift' and Jeannette."

"That's about the size of it," she whispered thickly.

"Okay, look." He halted and held up a hand, laughing a little as the irony of what he was doing hit him. "This is weird," he muttered, half to himself. "Isn't it the guy that's supposed to be skittish about commitments?"

He rubbed a hand over the intractable stubble of his hair, then across his eyes, which had begun to burn. "I know the odds aren't good for cops, but also I know some who've beaten them. And Jeannette seems to have become my responsibility whether you wanted her to or not. As for your…other thing, I guess I don't quite get what the problem is."

She dashed at one eye with her fingertips, sniffed, then laughed softly. "I can't believe this is happening. I never meant for it to, I swear. I thought—" She drew in a breath, put her hands on her knees and straightened her back. "I want The Gift—The Curse, whatever you want to call it— to end with me. It has to end…with me."

Wade shook his head in puzzlement, distracted by the sweet gentle curve of her spine above the sagging drape of sheet, and the alluring promise of more treasures beneath it.

"Why are you so convinced being psychic is the kiss of death for a relationship? Hell, if it's passing it on you're afraid of, we can always just use birth control." He added that in a rough, determined voice, ruthlessly squelching the voice of instinct somewhere deep inside him that had jumped up in immediate protest.

What? No kids? What about family? Hold on a minute here!

Having felt his longing, Tierney just smiled at him and shook her head. "Oh, Wade. I wish it were that simple, I really do."

"It *is* that simple. If you want something badly enough you find a way to make it work."

Her mind filled with images of a sweet but stubborn child. Gently she said, "You hardly know me."

"Maybe I know you better than you'd like to think I do. And if I don't know you as well as I'd like to, that's on you." He stabbed a forefinger at her. "Yeah, Tee. You think I block you? *You* block *me*. You shut me out. And I don't know why, because I don't even have the ability to read people like you do. Maybe—" he paused, and his eyes narrowed as if they hurt him "—yeah, maybe that's what's really scaring you. The idea that you'd have to open yourself up to someone. Because that's what it takes to make a relationship work, you know—you have to let someone in. Let yourself be vulnerable. Need someone." His voice grew gruff. "Like I needed you last night. Like you needed me when your grandmother was missing. Only in a relationship it's not just once in a while, it's all the time, twenty-four-seven. That's what makes it work. You open up for each other. You trust. You share."

She couldn't answer him; her throat was locked up tight. After a moment, with his luminous blue eyes looking deep into hers, he said softly, "So, it can be done, Miss Tee. Which I guess makes the question, do you *want* a relationship with me? At all?"

Yes...oh, yes. More than I could have believed possible.

She swallowed and looked away.

"Ha!" Wade's finger traced her spine, devastating her with goose bumps. "You do, don't you? I knew it. You're not the only one who can—"

She whirled on him, tears smarting in her eyes—angry tears this time. "For God's sake, Wade, use your head. Look at my family. Haven't you noticed the complete and total absence of *men?* We're a family of single women. Doesn't that tell you something?"

He simply looked at her, eyes tender, his smile, even clothed in morning stubble, angelic.

She wanted to throttle him.

"Jeannette, my mother, me—"

"You...are young, my dear—you just haven't found the right person yet. *Hadn't.* Until now. You don't know whether your mother's single or not, and anyway, you can hardly blame The Gift if she is, since she doesn't even have it. Jeannette, from what you told me, wasn't married long enough to know how it would have worked out."

"But that's just it—Gran never tried again. Want to know why? She was afraid to." Words tumbled out of her, faster than she could think, faster than she could screen them. "Because she believed she should have prevented Tommy's death. She told me. She believed her Gift didn't work with him, that it actually prevented her from being able to see the danger. She was afraid to let herself get that close to anyone again. She thought...she thought—" But the freshet of words had dried up.

Understanding bloomed in Wade's eyes. He said slowly, "So that's why you won't let yourself get close to me? You're afraid you might put me in some kind of danger?"

He gave a short bark of laughter. "God, I can't believe the irony of this. Isn't it the other way around? Seems to me it's my job that's put *you* in danger. You were brought in to help with my case, and *now* look. You've got a sadistic psychopath after you."

"Okay." She grabbed a desperate breath. "Okay, back to *your* job, since you mention it. What about the way this…whatever it is between us—"

"Relationship," he offered, eyes narrowed.

"Well, what about the way it's affecting your job?"

Slam went his shields, but not before she caught a glimmer of guilt. Guilt mixed with bright flashes of fear.

"What the hell do you mean?"

She got up, adjusting the sheet around herself, and he let her go, perhaps both of them needing the distance, both physical and emotional, like a moat between them.

She faced him across the chasm and said gently, "Wade, you're here right now, aren't you? Here with me. Where would you normally be on the morning after finding a killer's private lair?"

He leaned back on one elbow, outwardly relaxed, eyes wary. And not even a hint of emotion sneaking past his barricades. "Oh, sifting through a mountain of evidence, probably. Trying to figure out the creep's whereabouts. His next move. Next—"

"Victim?" She paused, and the word hung shimmering between them. Softly she added, "But you know his next victim, don't you, Wade."

"Yeah, and I've got her in protective custody." His lips stretched in a smile. "With some obvious variations, I'd be doing the same if it were anyone else."

"Would you? Truthfully?" Again she waited before quietly adding, "You know who the killer wants, you know where she—"

He shifted irritably, sat upright. "No. Don't even think—"

"I am thinking. It's you who's refusing to admit what needs to be done. Because you have…feelings for me, Wade. Because of those feelings, you're not doing your job."

His hands gripped the edge of the mattress and his eyes hardened. "Don't tell me how to do my job." His voice was low and dangerous.

She could feel her heart thumping beneath her arms where they crisscrossed her body, holding the sheet in place. "If it was anyone but me, you'd have it in motion already. You know you would. It's a no-brainer. You have a chance to catch this guy, and you're not taking it."

"Tee, I'm warning you."

"Wade." She closed her eyes, sucked in a breath. "I was brought in to help solve this case. Now I have a chance to help you close it. Please, let me do it."

He got up slowly but in a fury, like magma rising. "Goddamn it, Tierney, I'm not going to let you be some sort of bait. Like a…a lamb staked out for a tiger. Don't ask me to, because I won't do it."

"I know," she said, shaking so hard she could feel her teeth chattering. Now that the moment was here, she was terrified. "That's why I didn't ask you."

Wade felt ice creep around his heart. "What are you talking about?"

She lifted her chin and met his eyes, standing her ground in the face of his anger without flinching. And angry as he was with her just then, he had to admit her courage humbled him. As the words he dreaded tore at his heart.

"I called your boss. Yesterday. Nola Hoffman, isn't that her name? Anyway, she thinks it's a great idea. So does her boss…Styles? It's already in the works, Wade. You're going to use me to smoke out your killer."

In the lakeshore house in South Carolina, Cory Pearson closed the lid of his overnighter—the one he'd just brought back with him from Lebanon—and zipped it shut. He looked at his wife, sitting cross-legged in the middle of the bed, somberly watching him. "You know I wish I didn't have to leave again so soon. I just—"

"You don't have to explain to me, Pearse."

He leaned across the suitcase to kiss her. "I know. But just the same. This trip—losing my cameraman—it really brought it home to me." He smiled crookedly. "As if I needed any more reminding after that little adventure of ours in the Philippines. How things can change in a heartbeat—literally. Change forever. I've come this close, now I'm starting to get superstitious. What if something happened to one or the other of us, and we never got a chance to know each other? I don't know if I could handle it, Sam."

His wife bounced her way off the bed and came to put her arms around him. Hugged him close for a long, precious time. Then she stepped away from him, and in a resolute voice made poignant by her smile and the tears shining in her eyes, said, "You've got a plane to catch, Pearse. Go. And be sure and call me after. The very minute. Promise."

"I promise. I love you so damn much, Samantha June."

"I know."

* * *

The silence in the car was profound. Wade had wrapped himself in it like a survivor of some disaster huddled in a blanket, refusing to even look at the woman sitting mute and motionless as a statue beside him.

He drove with the window down and his elbow propped on the sill, his hand covering the lower part of his face, while he went over the plan again in his mind.

It was simple enough, on its face.

The department would "leak" word to the media—through its usual channels—that another body had been found, believed to be the work of the Torture Killer. The location of the crime scene would also be leaked. The idea being that the TK, James Jeffrey Larson, knowing himself to be innocent of this particular crime, but knowing also that his designated next victim—Tierney—would likely be present at the crime scene, would make every possible effort to show up there, as well. Ideally he would be spotted and taken down on the spot. Failing that, Larson would, hopefully, follow her from the crime scene, waiting for his chance.

Which police would make every effort to give him.

The variables, and thus the possibilities for something to go wildly wrong, were legion. Certainties were few.

Consequently, Wade was furious. Not to mention worried. And scared out of his mind.

None of which he made any attempt to keep Tierney from reading, along with the fact that he considered her to be stubborn, intractable, foolhardy and…some things he couldn't even think of words for.

Tierney bore all this without flinching. She ached with

his suffering, understood it even though she believed strongly that he was wrong.

She'd tried her best to reassure him.

"I'll be perfectly safe, Wade. Remember, this isn't a killer who strikes from a distance, or from cover. He needs to be up close and personal with his victim."

"What," he'd answered back, "you're telling me my job, again? I know what he does when he gets 'up close and personal with his victims, remember? I've seen them—all of them. You've only seen one—in person. But hey—I've got pictures. Maybe you need to take a good, close look."

She replied gently, knowing the cruelty was only a measure of his deep concern for her. "The point is, there should be plenty of time for police to close in before he has a chance to hurt me."

"*Should.* That's the word. No guarantees."

"Also, don't forget I'll be able to 'feel' him if he even gets close. I'll be wired, Wade. I'll be able to warn you when he's nearby."

"Yeah?" His eyes had bored into hers, red-rimmed, brilliant as diamonds. "What if he blocks you? This guy knows what you can do. He believes in what you can do so much, he wants to kill you to protect himself."

"He may try to block his emotions, but I don't think he'll be able to, not completely. The emotions driving this man are simply too powerful. He can't control them. If he could, he probably wouldn't be doing these terrible things."

Wade shifted suddenly, jerking himself upright in the driver's seat.

"I can't believe you're going to do this." He smacked

the steering wheel with his fist. "Damn it, Tee—you've been inside this guy's head."

Her thoughts had been wandering wistfully back over their more tender moments, and she had to clear her throat before she could reply. "Soul, not head."

"Even worse. You *know* how sick he is."

She shook her head, sadness making that her only possible response for a moment. Then she said softly, "Not sick—damaged. Beyond repair, probably, but I don't think he was born that way. This was done to him."

"I can't believe it," Wade said to the windshield, lips stretched in a travesty of a smile. "Now she's actually feeling sympathy for the guy."

And again, knowing where it came from, she forgave the dig with a small shrug and a wry smile. "I can't help it, you know. It's the price you pay for having empathy."

He didn't reply, and the car once again filled with silence.

Empathy. Wade was beginning to hate that word. Curse the day he'd first heard it. What did it mean, anyhow? It *seemed* to mean, to him anyway, that having it would make it damn near impossible to know for sure how to feel about anything.

He considered himself a pretty fair-minded, liberal-thinking kind of guy—for a cop—but how in the hell was he supposed to do his job if the perp's point of view kept getting in the way? He wasn't supposed to understand the dirtbag's motivation, just catch the sonofabitch and put him away.

Beside him, Tierney stirred restlessly, and because he was already on edge, fully aware he'd been broadcasting and itching for a fight, he barked at her. *"What?"*

She turned her head toward him and gave him a long look. He didn't have to see her expression for it to make him feel uncomfortable.

He wondered, after what he'd said to her about relationships being about sharing, being open with each other, whether she'd answer him now at all. Or, if she did, with her favorite evasion. *Nothing.*

Thinking about that made him feel bleaker…sadder. More lonely than he'd ever been before.

And then she said softly, "Did you ever think…if only a few things had gone differently for James Jeffrey Larson—or for you—that it could be you out there, the hunted…and he with the badge, the hunter?"

He exhaled in an explosion of shock. "My God. Is that what you think? That I could—"

"He was abandoned…abused. Terribly. So were you."

"*What?* I never was. What gave you—"

"Wade, I was with you—remember? There, in your nightmare. I know how terrified you were. How traumatized. If you hadn't had someone—"

"Someone? *Who?* I can't remember anyone being there. It was a *dream,* for God's sake. Hell, the guy—angel, whatever—probably wasn't even real. A figment of my imagination."

"If he was," Tierney said in her quiet, unarguable way, "you invented him because you needed to. Proof enough right there that your situation must have been intolerable. We all have ways of coping, Wade. Some people's personalities fracture into separate pieces, some develop into monsters themselves. Some simply choose to forget."

* * *

Cory's plane touched down in Portland in clear weather, hazy sunshine and 81 degrees Fahrenheit, at shortly after one in the afternoon, local time. By the time he'd rented a car and checked into his hotel near the airport it was almost two-thirty.

Which made it nearly dinner time on the east coast— and the middle of the night in the Middle East, which was probably closer to the time his body clock was on. He was definitely getting hungry. The first thing he did when he got to his room, however, was dump his suitcase on the extra bed and take out his cell phone. The number for Portland police headquarters was already stored in the phone's memory. He keyed it in, pressed the call button and, when the polite voice answered, asked to speak to Detective Callahan in homicide.

"Yes, sir…is this an emergency?"

"No. It's, uh, personal."

"I'm sorry, sir, Detective Callahan is in the field. Would you like his voice mail?"

"Sure," Cory said.

He waited for the connection, then left the message. "Uh…yes, Detective Callahan, this is Cory Pearson, the journalist you, uh…we met last week at the Rose Garden? I wonder if you'd give me a call, please?"

He left his cell-phone number and, after a pause, added, "It's important."

He disconnected, then sat for a few minutes on the edge of the bed, nerves twitching with unexpended adrenaline. He was familiar enough with police departments to know what "in the field" meant, and he figured his chances of

Detective Callahan calling him back any time soon were pretty slim.

A growl of protest from his midsection reminded him he should probably go get himself something to eat before he did anything else. After that…

Well, he still had the man's address. Maybe he wouldn't wait for that phone call. Maybe he'd just drive on up to Wade's place like he'd done once before and wait for him there.

"Well, so much for that," Wade said grimly as the car sped away from the anthill of activity centered around the staged crime scene. "The line's in the water, now let's see if this creep bites."

After much discussion, it had been decided to place the crime scene in a remote but easily accessible industrial park on the outskirts of the city, several miles upriver on the Willamette. This, it was thought, would provide enough cover for the suspected killer to observe the scene without being scared off, as well as plenty of drive time back to the city to allow him to pick up his quarry's trail, without making it seem too easy for him—too much like a setup.

The crime scene itself, with a young female patrol officer playing the part of the victim, had been gruesomely and graphically real, but it hadn't bothered Tierney as much as she'd expected. Due to the absence of emotions, of course, both residual and present. The CSIs and detectives on the scene were pretty good actors, but their gut feelings had known the difference.

Naturally, Wade hadn't been happy about any of it. All through the planning and execution stages, his anger had been like the constant shriek of electronic feedback inside

Tierney's head. Now they were driving home by a meander-
ing route meant to make it easy for Larson to follow, and at
the same time, give Tierney plenty of opportunity to "make"
him. But she was having a hard time "hearing" anything
except the pounding of her headache and the discordant
noise that was Wade's all-consuming fear for her safety.

She wished she could say something to him, something
that would reassure him or make him understand what his
revved-up emotions were doing to her and get him to block
them—or at least dial them down a notch. But this time the
words wouldn't come. Her own emotions seemed to have
gotten away from her and were all over the place, creating
havoc in her mind. She felt too exhausted, right now, for
another emotional battle with Wade.

And confused. Because, as they drew nearer to the
city, she began picking up glimmers of what she believed
might be the killer—his intense focus on her, his avid excitement. But, strangely, without the equally intense rage
she'd expected.

Could it be that now he had her in his sights, he was so
intent on carrying out his agenda that he'd put his rage on
hold? She tried to home in on the impression, but thanks
to her headache and the persistent background noise of her
own and Wade's emotions, she wasn't able to receive
anything clearly.

And then, further complicating things, back on familiar
streets, she began to hear a new voice in the mix. No, not
new—one she'd heard before. One she recognized.

Now she sat tense as wire, hands clasped in her lap to
keep from inadvertently making some motion that would
prompt Wade to ask his inevitable question. *What?*

If he did, what would she answer? That she was almost sure The Watcher was back? How could she tell him what she wasn't even sure of herself? Especially given that Wade wasn't as convinced as she was that The Watcher was benign, and in his current frame of mind he might easily jump to the wrong conclusion.

She began to feel increasingly edgy and chilled, balanced on the edge of panic, like a small prey animal lost in unfamiliar darkness.

The predator was out there…somewhere. Somewhere close. She could feel him. She'd been given all the defenses she needed to elude him, outwit him, defeat him. But now, as the danger grew closer, deep inside she felt the fear…the confusion…the doubt.

All those defenses… Would they be enough?

Chapter 12

Tierney noticed when Wade made the turn that would take him up the hill into his own neighborhood instead of toward hers, and he was so intent on his own thoughts it was a shock when she straightened up like she'd been stung.

And an even greater shock, after the deafening silence in the car for the past half hour, when she actually spoke.

"Where are we going? I thought—"

He smiled without an ounce of humor. "Yeah, I know the plan is to drive you home, pretend Jeannette's gone wandering off again...and off we go to the park to look for her."

This was the part of the plan he dreaded, the part where he and Tierney were supposed to split up to search the park. Which was supposed to give the killer his chance. Thinking about it now, he swore silent blasphemies, wondering at what point he'd lost his mind and agreed to go along with this insanity. Sure, supposedly there would be cops stationed undercover all over that damn park. But he, better than anybody, knew how the best-laid plans could turn bad.

"I'm going to stop by my place first, if you don't mind." His voice was a quiet but dangerous growl. "Pick up my mail and a change of clothes." And the backup weapon he wasn't supposed to carry, and which nearly all detectives did. He'd never had to use one, but he knew he'd feel better having it. He sure as hell didn't want to be caught without his weapon the one time he needed it.

It occurred to him then that she'd looked deathly pale, in the one quick glance he'd given her in the darkening car. He felt a painful stab of guilt and concern. He probably wasn't making this any easier for her, letting his dislike of this whole bait-the-tiger plan boil over the way he had. He hadn't been blocking the way he felt about her, either.

He pulled into his driveway, looked over at her and said contritely, "Hey, you okay? Getting any bad vibes?"

She looked him straight in the eye and said, "No."

Well, she told herself, it was the truth—the vibes she was getting weren't bad—not at all.

There was tremendous excitement and anticipation, all mixed up with intense anxiety. The emotions were rolling in on her in waves, from opposite directions, like weather fronts colliding, one benign, the other malevolent. *Good and evil...*

How would she know which was which, and which direction it was coming from? She felt paralyzed with panic. *Gran! Where are you? Please hear me. I need you!*

"Well," Wade said, "I'm not about to leave you in the car. Not this time." He got out and slammed his door, head moving from side to side like a radar antenna, scanning the street as he went around to open hers.

She got out, moving like a robot, her mind filled with the thunder of those two massive, inexorable forces…

When a car door slammed across the street, she didn't even hear it.

Wade heard it. He whirled, shoving Tierney behind him. His weapon was already in his hands.

On the other side of the street a shadowy figure was moving toward him. Wade couldn't believe it—the dirtbag was going to make his move right here! It was his worst-case scenario, the reason he'd had no faith in this so-called plan. Reminded him of something he'd heard somewhere. *You want to make God laugh? Make a plan.*

He was already in his take-down crouch, weapon aimed and ready. "James Larson—stop right there!"

"Wait—" The figure extended his arms. Too dark to tell if he had a weapon. "I'm not—"

"Whoever you are—take one more step and I'll be forced to shoot. Don't make me do it…"

Hell, yeah. Make my day…

"Look, it's not what you think."

The man's voice—for an instant, Wade thought it sounded familiar. Hard to tell—it was high with fear and shook with nervous laughter. Uncertain now, he hesitated…turned to look at Tierney, trying to get her take on this guy.

She seemed frozen…eyes wide with terror. It was all the confirmation he needed.

"Down on the ground—*now!*"

The figure folded slowly to his knees, but his arms were

still outstretched in entreaty. "Wade—wait—my name is Cory Pearson. We've met before. I just want to talk to you. For God's sake—I'm your brother!"

Rage blew through Wade's head, turning his vision red and his voice to ice.

"Yeah? Well, you just made the worst mistake of your life, pal. Now I know you're a liar. I've only got one brother. His name's Matthew, not Cory. Lives in San Diego. In a wheelchair. That's right—he's a paraplegic, goddamn you. Now, get down on the ground! Lace your fingers together—hands behind your head! Come on—do it. Face on the ground! *Do it—now!*"

Tierney watched Wade dart into the street and drop to one knee beside the figure lying prone on the ground. The figure of the man who claimed to be Wade's brother. But…could this be right? Was this the killer, after all?

Her head hurt. Felt like it was going to explode. She felt so many emotions, so many intense conflicting emotions!

Fear…surprise…glee…menace…triumph…fury…despair!

She felt like a dazed rabbit completely surrounded by wolves. Paralyzed…helpless.

In the center of the maelstrom only one thought came to her. Her grandmother's voice, trembling with grief. *I saw, but I wouldna' believe.*

She understood that now, as if a spotlight shone brightly on the words and images in her head. Understood how Jeannette could have "known" about her beloved's peril, but still be unable to prevent it.

It was, truly, what made The Gift a curse.

Gran…please help me. I need you!

The answer came at last, and she almost didn't hear it. *Don't listen so hard, darling.*

But the voice inside her mind wasn't Jeannette's. That voice had been crystalline and bright, like water laughing over pebbles. This was a voice she didn't recognize, and yet...had she heard it before? Somewhere...faint, like a whisper...nostalgic, like the softest of breezes on a warm spring morning, bringing with it the scent of lilacs.

Relax...let it pour over you... Like rain. You'll know...

Tierney's heart leaped with new hope. *Gran?*

Again the soft breeze, a hint of laughter. *Not quite...*

She reached out to the voice, incredulous...disbelieving... *Mother? But you didn't—you don't...*

I've always been able to hear you, Tee.

"Momma?" She said it out loud, in a voice tremulous with tears.

Wade heard it and turned toward her. Too late.

To Cory, it seemed to happen in a second. Less. From his position, flat on his belly in the street with his cheek pressing into the gritty and still warm pavement, he saw a shadowy form lunge from the shadows between the trees and parked cars that lined the street. Saw him grab Tierney from behind and envelop her in an evil parody of an embrace—the same one with which he'd surprised his wife last night, on his return from Beirut.

The pressure on his spine vanished, as Wade sprang up and started for the pair at a dead run—only to come to a dead stop an instant later, hands stretched at his sides like outriggers to help halt his forward momentum.

A moment later Cory saw what Wade had seen first—

the glint of a knife pressed against Tierney's throat. And something else in the man's other hand. A gun. Small, deadly...and pointed straight at Wade.

This was Cory's worst nightmare. Had it been a premonition? Superstition? Either way, his greatest fear—that he would find his lost brother only to lose him forever at the final moment—was coming true.

Shouts flew back and forth through the twilight.

The voice of a killer, high and taut, sobbing with fear and resolve. "Put the gun down, *now!* I'll kill her, I swear I will—"

"Don't do it—I'm warning—"

"I'll kill her right here. I'll cut her throat..."

"Wade! He means it, man. Don't do anything stupid—"

"Okay...okay. Look! I'm putting the gun down. Just... don't hurt her. Don't...hurt her."

Tierney was overwhelmed by the emotions. The sheer brutality of them, like hammer blows inside her head. Battering her. Destroying her. How much more of this could she take?

Desperately she clung to sanity, and her lifelines were the only clear thoughts she could find in the midst of the chaos.

The Watcher, Cory...he's who he says he is. He's Wade's brother!

Wade loves me, more than he does his own life.

And I love him the same.

And this man...with the knife I feel cutting into my throat and the gun pointed straight at Wade...he means to kill us both.

Then...incredibly, another "voice" swelled inside her mind, another voice to cling to in the terror of the moment.

This one she'd heard before. No words, just feelings. Simple and direct.

Love! Devotion! Defend! Protect!

She realized that she was moving backward, that she was being forced, half-dragged down the sidewalk. She could feel the warm trickle of blood down her neck and between her breasts.

She heard the sound of a man's ragged breathing and a high-pitched keening inside her head. The sound of fear and rage coming rapidly to a boil.

She heard a click—incredibly loud and outside her head—and even though she'd never heard the sound before, she knew it. The sound of a gun getting ready to fire.

And she couldn't move, couldn't do anything to stop what she knew was going to happen.

She kept moving…backward…the pressure on her throat unbearable. Darkness swam into the edges of her vision. She heard Wade's voice, rough with anguish.

"Come on, don't, man—don't—"

In utter desperation, her mind screamed, *Bruno!*

In the next instant she was falling backward.

There was an explosion—the gun! So close it seemed to be everywhere—inside her mind, outside her body. But she wasn't deafened by it, not completely—she could hear other sounds—scuffles, grunts of effort, screams of fury, wordless shouts and cries of pain.

And then…nothing. Darkness. Finally. And blessed, blessed silence.

Cory saw the man go down—inexplicably—taking his hostage with him. And almost simultaneously he heard the gunshot. Felt the concussion of it as if in his own body. He was already on his feet when he saw Wade crumple to the ground.

He'd been in enough life and death situations to know what he had to do first, and he did it without hesitation, even while his mind was screaming in agony. He darted across the street to where the shooter lay momentarily stunned, half under the body of the woman, who appeared to be unconscious. He kicked the gun away from the man's hand and sent it spinning across the driveway, then stomped down on the wrist of the hand holding the knife. Breathing hard, he bent down and felt for the woman's pulse.

Somewhere behind him, like the sound of a cavalry charge in the darkest hour, he could hear Wade swearing and groaning. Shouting at him.

"Is she all right? Did he hurt her?"

When Cory didn't reply immediately, being somewhat preoccupied with getting the knife out of its owner's reach and the man away from his intended victim, Wade almost screamed, "Answer me, goddamn it!"

Breathing hard, Cory yelled back, "She's okay I think—just fainted." He rolled the assailant, unresisting now and sobbing like a child, onto his stomach and planted one knee in the small of his back. And was finally able to ask the question he most desperately wanted the answer to. "How 'bout you? Where did he get you?"

"In my damn leg," Wade croaked, and started to laugh, the way someone does when he's in unspeakable pain. "I'll be okay…if somebody…will just get this…stinking dog off of me."

Cory twisted around to look at him, lying on his back

at the bottom of the driveway. In the fading light he could see that his brother's arms were flung over his face in a vain attempt to protect it from the attentions of the enormously obese basset hound that was sprawled on his chest.

That was the first thing Tierney saw when she opened her eyes, though it took her a moment or two to realize what she was seeing. But yes, it was Bruno, his front half flopped across Wade's body, and he was bathing Wade's face with a long, floppy—no doubt very wet—tongue.

Clammy and crying—but laughing, too—she crawled over to the two of them, not sure which one to gather into her arms first.

The decision resolved itself when she saw the dark stain under Wade's body, growing larger as she watched. "Oh God, Wade, you're *hurt*. Where—"

"My leg—I think. Bleeding like a sonofagun, but…I'll be all right. Just please, get this miserable mutt off me."

"He's just trying to tell you he's sorry you're hurt," she sobbed. "He didn't mean for that to happen."

He turned his head toward her, desperately trying to avoid the dog's ministrations. In a much weaker voice, he rasped, "He got me *shot*."

"He saved my life," Tierney said as she pulled Bruno into her arms and hugged him.

Love! Adoration! Utter and complete devotion!

"Fair trade," Wade whispered. "Any day."

The cops arrived moments later, followed by a whole host of emergency personnel. With the prisoner in custody, finally relieved of his guard duty, Cory walked over to Wade, who was now strapped onto a gurney with a mask on his face and an IV bag dripping fluids into one arm. The other had been claimed by the blond woman, who clung to his hand as if she'd never let go.

Momentarily at a loss for words, Cory reached out and grasped his brother's shoulder. Wade tried his best to speak, but was too weak from pain and loss of blood to make himself understood through the oxygen mask.

Cory gulped back a dry sob, bent down close to him and said huskily, "Shh…It's okay…it's gonna be okay. You're safe now. It's okay…"

Above the mask, Wade's eyes grew wide with wonder. He clawed at the plastic, managed to pull it away. "I know you," he croaked. "The voice in my dream. It's you. It was you. You're 'The Protector.'"

"Yeah, that's me," Cory said, ignoring the tears running down his face. "Some protector I am. I couldn't…I couldn't stop them. Man, I'm so sorry. They took you—"

Wade, too weak—or too emotional—for words, simply groped for his hand.

"Hey, guys…we need to take him now."

Cory looked up and nodded at the paramedics standing ready to heave the gurney into the ambulance. He squeezed his brother's hand, then moved aside. The blonde bent down to kiss Wade, then she, too, stepped back, out of the way. As the ambulance doors closed, she reached blindly for Cory's hand.

He slipped his arm around her shoulders and pulled her close, pressed a brotherly kiss to the top of her head, then murmured, "Come on—the hospital. I'll drive, you tell me the way. I'm Wade's brother, by the way. Cory Pearson."

She dashed away tears, then smiled and held out her

hand. "I know. I met you in the Rose Gardens that day, remember? I'm Tierney Doyle. Soon to be your sister-in-law. I think."

Oh, but in her heart, she *knew*.

It was much later that night, after the surgery and assurances from the doctors that Wade would recover completely from his wound, given time. Cory had offered to give Tierney a ride home, if she wanted to go.

She didn't, of course. She'd arranged for Clair Yee to stay with Jeannette until further notice. With the arrest of the Torture Killer, the security guard had been relieved of duty.

"Thanks," she told Cory, curling into the chair next to Wade's bed. "I think I'll stay here." In truth, there wasn't any place else she wanted to be. Ever. "You go ahead, though. Get some rest. I know you have a lot to talk about, but he'll be more able to…tomorrow."

Cory nodded, hesitated, stood gazing for a long moment at the man snoring quietly in the hospital bed, stubbled face dark against the pillows. His face flinched ever so slightly, and he threw Tierney a look of apology. "Sorry…I understand you're an empath. I must be coming on pretty strong right now."

She smiled sleepily at him. "It's okay. The kind of emotions I'm getting from you are like…balm. They heal me." Her voice broke and she lowered her face onto her arms for a brief moment. When she lifted it again, she caught Cory tiptoeing away.

"Oh, wait—Cory…"

He turned back, his face kind, eyes warm and bright. "Yes?"

"How did you do it?" She nodded toward the man she'd come to adore so completely in so short a time. "How did you find him?"

Cory's smile was wry. "Wish I could claim the credit. I hired a private investigator—great guy. His name's Holt Kincaid. Specializes in finding people."

He paused, fighting it. But he was a journalist, after all. "If you don't mind my asking...why?"

She took a breath. Lifted her face, ignoring the tears that had begun to roll freely down her cheeks. "I think," Tierney said as she gave him her most radiant smile, "I'd like to find my mother."

Epilogue

Wade dialed the phone from his hospital bed. He closed his eyes as he counted the rings, but it didn't help to shut out the image of his brother the way he'd last seen him, making his way slowly and awkwardly through his apartment in his wheelchair.

It never did.

The rings stopped after only two, surprising the hell out of him. Always before when he'd called, it had taken at least six rings for Matt to get to the phone.

"Man," he said, "that was fast."

"Cell phone," his brother said. "Who's this?"

"It's me—Wade. How are you, buddy?"

"Hey...Wade. Wow—been a while."

"Yeah." He gritted his teeth against a double whammy of pain waves, one from his leg, suspended in a sling and swathed in surgical dressings, the other in his heart. Pure guilt. "Listen, about that—"

"Forget it, bro. It's cool. I understand. So…how you been? Bad guys keepin' you busy?"

Wade laughed—tried to do it without moving anything that might hurt. "Yeah, well…I guess I've been better. But, hey—that's not why I called. I've got somebody here wants to talk to you." He paused. "You sitting down?"

"Oh, yeah, funny. Very funny. So who is it? Hey—don't tell me. You got married?"

Wade looked up at Tierney, reached for her hand and squeezed it tightly. "Not quite," he said in a voice gone raspy with emotions. "Not yet. Soon though. We want you to be there. And I promise you, man, you're gonna love her. No—this is…" He paused, looked up at the faces bending over him and muttered half to himself, "Jeez, I didn't think this was going to be so hard… Uh, Mattie? Remember those nightmares I used to have? I told you about it, remember? There was this voice—you said it was—"

"An angel. Sure, I remember. I was a kid, what can I say? So? What about it?"

Wade took a deep breath and grinned up at Cory, who was standing poised, his face a mask of suspense that didn't come close to hiding his emotions. Tierney, unable to hold hers in any longer, lowered her tear-drenched face to his chest, and he let his fingers come to rest in her soft, soft curls and found the strength he needed to continue.

"Well, little brother…guess what? He's real. And here he is. In person." His voice broke and he barely got the rest of it out. "Mattie—say hello to our angel…the brother you didn't know you had."

* * * * *

Mills & Boon® Intrigue
brings you a sneak preview of…

Jessica Andersen's Doctor's Orders

Mandy Sparks always had a difficult time
following orders under chief surgeon Parker
Radcliffe. But when one of Mandy's patients dies
unexpectedly, the two have only two days to find a
cure. But spending time together could have more
seductive consequences than they imagined…

Don't miss this thrilling new story available next
month in Mills & Boon® Intrigue.

Doctor's Orders

by

Jessica Andersen

"I'm sorry, Doctor, but Ms. Dulbecco died early this morning." On the phone, the nurse's voice softened. "Did you know her personally?"

Mandy Sparks gripped the handset tightly and turned her back on the chaos of the Emergency Services Department, so her coworkers—or one coworker in particular—wouldn't see how badly the news had upset her. She looked down, and her long blond hair fell forward past her face, forming another barrier between her and the rest of Boston General. "I didn't know her well. She was a patient, that's all."

But to Mandy there was no "that's all" about it. As far as she was concerned, every case was special, every injury or illness a personal battle.

"She went peacefully," the nurse offered, as though that made a difference. And in a way, it did. Mandy hadn't been able to pinpoint the cause of Irene Dulbecco's pain, but she'd been able to make the forty-something mother of two more comfortable. She'd gotten Irene stabilized, and had sent her upstairs to the Urgent Care Department, where her husband and kids could visit more easily. Then, Mandy had gone home and crashed for six hours of badly needed sleep.

Logically she knew the staff members in Urgent Care were the best at what they did, but now she wondered if things would've gone differently if she'd stayed.

"If there's nothing else, Doctor…" the nurse said, drawing out the last word to indicate that it was time for her to move on to the next call.

It wasn't just her, either. The prevailing motto at BoGen these days seemed to be "move 'em in and push 'em out, and don't get emotionally attached," which Mandy found more than a little disturbing. Or maybe she was painting everyone else with a brush that belonged strictly to the department head, Parker Radcliff.

As far as she was concerned, Radcliff pretty much embodied the word *disturbing*.

"That's all," Mandy finally said into the phone. "Thanks for—" She broke off when the nurse disconnected before she'd finished, but kept the phone pressed to her ear for a moment longer, in order to buy herself some time to regroup.

I shouldn't have come back here, she thought, closing her eyes and pinching the bridge of her nose in an effort to delay the incipient headache. *I should've taken the job in Michigan.*

Unfortunately the smaller hospital in Ann Arbor had lacked the clout of Boston General, and Mandy needed at least another eighteen months of top-flight E.R. experience and a solid recommendation if she wanted a shot at winning next year's Meade Fellowship. With good E.R. openings in short supply, she'd been very lucky that her previous employment at BoGen had automatically moved her ahead of the other applicants.

Now, though, barely a month into her second stint at the hospital, she was starting to think she'd made a big mistake.

"Are you going to stand there listening to the dial tone all morning, Dr. Sparks?" Radcliff's voice said unexpectedly from directly behind her, interrupting her thoughts with the sarcasm he seemed to save just for her. "Or were you planning on seeing patients at some point today?"

Mandy stiffened, but forced herself not to stammer and retreat. Instead she took a deep breath, tossed her hair back from her face and turned toward the man she'd once—in a bout of youth and stupidity—thought she loved.

Radcliff's wavy, dark brown hair was tipped with silver at his temples, and faint creases fanned out from his dark blue eyes. Those small signs of mortality should've made him seem approachable, but the square set of his jaw and the coolness in his eyes formed an impenetrable barrier. He wore a crisp white lab coat, its breast pocket embroidered not with his name or title, but with two words: The Boss.

On any other man it might've been a joke.

On Radcliff, it was simple fact.

Four years ago, she'd been a lowly resident and he'd been the head attending, and ten years her senior. Now he ran the entire E.R., and spent more time on paperwork than medicine, which was lucky for her, because it had allowed her to avoid him since her return to BoGen. In turn, he'd limited their contact to snippy memos about increasing her patient turnover and keeping expensive tests to a minimum. On the few instances they'd been forced to interact face-to-face, they'd both made sure they were surrounded by a crowd of other staffers.

Until now.

Mandy's heart picked up a beat. "I was discussing a patient with Urgent Care. I saw her yesterday, and her symptoms didn't make sense to me. She passed away last night."

Radcliff glanced at his watch, sounding almost bored when he said, "She didn't die on your watch, which makes her Urgent Care's problem, not yours. And your shift started ten minutes ago."

Mandy couldn't believe he could be so callous about a patient's death. Sure, she'd heard the rumors that he'd only gotten colder over the past few years, but—

But nothing, her rational self interjected. *Don't think you know him now because you had a fling.*

Knowing that little voice inside her was right, darn it, she said, "Sorry. I'll skip one of my breaks or make up the time after my shift."

Whether she liked it or not, she needed Radcliff on her side when it came time for recommendation letters. Dr. Stewart Royal, chairman of the Meade Foundation, had warned her that the competition would be fierce. She was determined to win the all expenses paid year abroad, though. She'd dearly love to get her hands on the funding and support, which she'd use to travel to Shanghai and study traditional Chinese medicine—TCM—with the master of the art, Dr. Li Wong.

Rumor had it the foundation was getting ready to award this year's Meade Fellowship, but she held out little hope for her application. She needed another year of solid experience in her field of E.R. medicine, and a glowing recommendation from a heavy hitter like Parker Radcliff.

Which meant no picking fights with the boss, no matter how much his policies irritated her. No matter how much *he* irritated her.

He stared at her for a long moment, his eyes shadowed with suspicion, as if thinking she'd forget about making up the ten minutes the moment she was out of his range. Then, apparently deciding she was sincere, he nodded sharply. "See that you do.

And stop bothering Urgent Care. They have more important things to do than make you feel better about losing a patient."

"I wasn't bothering anyone. I—" Mandy snapped her mouth shut on the protest, but it was already too late.

"Yes, you were." He leaned in and reached for her, and for a mad, crazy second her heart thudded against her ribs at the thought that he was going to kiss her. Instead he plucked the phone handset from her fingers and hung it up with a decisive click. "Let it go."

FREE

2 BOOKS AND A SURPRISE GIFT!

We would like to take this opportunity to thank you for reading this Mills & Boon® book by offering you the chance to take TWO more specially selected titles from the Intrigue series absolutely FREE! We're also making this offer to introduce you to the benefits of the Mills & Boon® Book Club™—

- ★ **FREE home delivery**
- ★ **FREE gifts and competitions**
- ★ **FREE monthly Newsletter**
- ★ **Books available before they're in the shops**
- ★ **Exclusive Mills & Boon Book Club offers**

Accepting these FREE books and gift places you under no obligation to buy; you may cancel at any time, even after receiving your free shipment. Simply complete your details below and return the entire page to the address below. You don't even need a stamp!

YES! Please send me 2 free Intrigue books and a surprise gift. I understand that unless you hear from me, I will receive 4 superb new titles every month for just £3.19 each, postage and packing free. I am under no obligation to purchase any books and may cancel my subscription at any time. The free books and gift will be mine to keep in any case.

I9ZEE

Ms/Mrs/Miss/Mr...Initials ....
BLOCK CAPITALS PLEASE

Surname ....

Address ....

....

....Postcode ....

Send this whole page to:
The Mills & Boon Book Club, FREEPOST CN81, Croydon, CR9 3WZ